House
of Special
Purpose

House of Special Purpose

ISBN: 978-1-7348524-8-6 (hardback)
          978-1-7348524-0-0 (paperback)
          978-1-7348524-1-7 (ebook)

Printed in the United States of America

House
of Special
Purpose

A Jeannie Loomis Novel

GARY J. ROSE

ALSO, BY GARY J. ROSE

Jeannie Loomis Novels

Ark of the Covenant –
Raid on the Church of Our Lady Mary of Zion

Star Chamber

Forgotten Plans

Non-fiction

Towards the Integration of Police Psychology
Techniques to Combat

Juvenile Delinquency in K-12 Classrooms.

Hitting Rock Bottom

How to Create a Public-School Military Academy

Teaching Inside the Walls

I am fortunate as a writer to be surrounded by a great support group of relatives and friends, who unknowingly, in each of their various ways, help me through those long months needed to complete a novel. Without their help, this book would not be possible.

Special thanks to Mike and Mary Lake and my mother, for volunteering the many hours needed to read the rough draft of my manuscript making valuable suggestions while doing so.

To John Maghuyop, thank you for another great formatting and cover design.

Finally, to my readers, I sincerely believe in my quote, "When you stop dreaming or using your imagination, you start to die. I hope the adventures of Special Agent Jeannie Loomis and her team will inspire you to dream and use your imagination.

Enjoy!

"The larger crimes are apt to be the simpler, for the bigger the crime, the more obvious, as a rule, is the motive."

— Sir Arthur Conan Doyle

Prologue

On the night and morning of July 16th – 17th, 1918, in the Ipatiev House, known as the House of Special Purpose in Yekaterinburg, Russia, the Russian Imperial Romanov family, consisting of Czar Nicholas II, his wife Empress Alexandra and their five children, Olga, Tatiana, Maria, Anastasia and their son Alexei and all those who chose to accompany them into imprisonment, were shot and bayoneted to death.

The scene of the assassinations was that of shock to the killers, not because of the shootings, clubbing and bayoneting, but because the bullets from their weapons bounced off their targets. Unbeknownst to them, the Empress had sown the Romanoff jewelry into the fabric of their undergarments which caused the assassins' bullets to ricochet. Once the killings were completed, the assassins were ordered to strip the bodies of the dead and turn all of the Romanoff gems to the Cheka, the secret police. The collection at that time was estimated at over $500 million.

In 1922, the Cheka discovered during an inventory that three of the most expensive items of jewelry had been stolen from the state vault. Those items were a sapphire tiara, a sapphire bracelet, and an emerald necklace. Suspicion fell on a Cheka officer who, while being detained and interrogated about the theft and whereabouts of the jewels, committed suicide. The trail of the missing items went cold.

Chapter One

The woman approached the podium and tapped on the microphone which drew the attention of everyone else in the large briefing room. Those that were still standing made their way to their seats.

"Good morning. My name is Gloria Jamerson and I am the director of Russian intelligence with the NSA. I want to thank you all for fighting the Washington D.C. traffic so that you could attend this briefing.

Jamerson seemed to fit the stereotype of a long time Washington bureaucrat and Clinton and Obama supporter. She wore, what Pinheiro felt, was a too casual attire for a professional, especially standing in front of a podium. She had a pair of worn slacks and a non-flattering blouse. Her hair needed a bleach job and some type of styling. Former President Clinton started this craze when he took office, sometimes appearing in public dressed in less than business casual, but Obama took it to a whole new level, rarely wearing a suit and tie while his wife dressed like a model for a thrift store.

Looking over her shoulder to make sure all of the other speakers were in their seats, she returned to the microphone. "The individuals behind me will introduce themselves when they are up here. They represent agencies of the FBI, Interpol, NSA, DHS, CIA, and the government of Russia."

Richard Pinheiro, an assistant director of the Department of Homeland Security, recognized many of the people behind Jamerson but not the person who seemed uneasy surrounded by individuals providing national security for the United States. "At least he was dressed in a suit and carried himself professionally," Pinheiro thought.

A large screen began descending from the ceiling to the right of the podium. Using a presenter, she pointed at a Mac resting of the podium. The screen showed a picture of an elderly man which most in the room instantly recognized as Anatoly Pavlenko. "Asshole," Pinheiro said to himself.

"If you don't recognize this man, his name is Anatoly Pavlenko. He was born in St. Petersburg, Russia, holds dual citizenship here in the U.S., and lives in this mansion in San Francisco (slide showing residence). The mansion was huge and Pinheiro knew it was located in the Pacific Heights area of the city, one of the most expensive areas in the United States.

The reference to San Francisco piqued the interest of Pinheiro. The DHS, NSA, SFPD, FBI, and surrounding law enforcement agencies of the bay area, recently concluded their investigation into the terrorist acts of three jihadist teams. Although one of the teams were successful in killing numerous Christians who had flocked to the Russian Orthodox Church in San Francisco, the other two teams were terminated before they could act. This was how he met FBI agent Jeannie Loomis, now his girlfriend. He now focused on what Agent Jamerson was presenting.

"Our agency, as well as the DHS, FBI, CIA, and Interpol believe, but cannot verify, that he funds most if not all of the left-wing anarchists including Antifa, with income from his holdings in the Ukraine and former Soviet Union satellite countries and Russia. He's into oil, gas, minerals and for the purpose of this briefing, stolen property."

With that she turned and nodded to one of the gentlemen seated behind her. He rose and started towards the podium. Wearing a black suit and red tie, Pinheiro thought that if you looked up Russian agent, you would find a picture of him displayed. He had to be an FSB agent surviving the change from the former secret police, the KGB.

"Good morning," he said, "or should I say Dobroye Utra?" He did not receive many laughs so he introduced himself. "My name is Vasili Sokalov. I am with the Russian State Department." Sure, you are, Pinheiro thought. He advanced to the next slide showing a picture of a male who obviously was royalty. "For those of you who never studied Russian history, this picture shows our last Czar of Russia, Nicholas II. He was our last czar because Lenin (slide advance) and the Red Army forced his abdication from the throne during our civil war in March 1917. (Slide advance) This is the former royal family of Czar Nicolas." Using the presenter and laser beam, he circled each of the individuals in the photo. "This is the Tsarina Alexandra, and these are their four daughters - Olga, Tatiana, Maria, and Anastasia. And this was to be the heir to the throne upon Czar Nicolas's death, the Tsarevich Alexei who was a hemophiliac."

(Slide advance) This is the Ipatiev House, or to say it correctly, it was the Ipatiev House since it no longer exists. It was called the House of Special Purpose and I will tell you why it was named this way if you do not already know. It was a merchant's house located in Yekaterinburg (later renamed Sverdlovsk) about 1,784 km from Moscow. This is where the former Emperor Nicholas II of Russia, his entire family, and members of his household were executed in July 1918 following the Bolshevik Revolution.

1 a.m. on July 17, 1918, the Romanovs were awakened by their personal physician Dr. Eugene Botkin who told them that they must dress and gather their belongings for a quick move to avoid the advancing White Army. The White armies, which supported the

tsar, were on the outside of the town's border and the boom of the big guns could already be heard.

Once dressed, they were escorted by this man, (slide advance) Yakov Yurovskhy,

leader of the secret police, the Cheka, who had been sent to guard the family after they had been placed in the Ipatiev House. They gathered in the cellar standing together almost as if they were posing for a family portrait. Alexandra, who was sick, asked for a chair, and Nicholas asked for another one for his only son, 13-year-old Alexei. Two were brought down to the room. They waited there until suddenly, 11 or 12 heavily armed men ominously came into the room. Yurovsky pulled a piece of paper from his pocket and read aloud the order given to him by the Ural Executive Committee:

"Nikolai Alexandrovich, in view of the fact that your relatives are continuing their attack on Soviet Russia, the Ural Executive Committee has decided to execute you."

"The Empress and Grand Duchess Olga, according to a guard's reminiscence, had tried to bless themselves, but failed amid the shooting. Yurovsky reportedly raised his Colt gun at Nicholas's torso and fired; Nicholas fell dead, pierced with at least three bullets in his upper chest. Another member of the killing squad shot and killed Alexandra with a bullet wound to the head. He then shot at Maria, who ran for the double doors, hitting her in the thigh. The remaining executioners shot chaotically over each other's shoulders until the room was so filled with smoke and dust that no one could see anything at all in the darkness nor hear any commands amid the noise. Within minutes, Yurovsky was forced to stop the shooting because of the caustic smoke of burned gunpowder and dust from the plaster ceiling caused by the reverberation of bullets, and the deafening gunshots. When they stopped, the doors were then opened to scatter the smoke. While waiting for the smoke to abate, the killers could hear moans and whimpers inside the room. As it cleared, it became evident that the czar, the czarina and several non-family members had been killed, all of the Imperial children were alive with only Maria injured."

Sokalov stopped talking and pulled a water bottle from under the podium and drank. He then replaced the bottle under the podium and continued. "The noise of the guns had been heard by households all around, awakening many people. The executioners were ordered to use their bayonets, a technique which proved ineffective and meant that the children had to be dispatched by still more gunshots, this time aimed more precisely at their heads. The Tsarevich was the first of the children to be executed. Yurovsky watched in disbelief as one of the killers spent an entire magazine from his Browning gun on Alexei, who was still seated transfixed in his chair; he also had jewels sewn into his undergarment and forage cap. The killer continued to shoot and stabbed him, and when that failed, Yurovsky shoved him aside and killed the boy with a gunshot to the head. The last to die were Tatiana, Anastasia, and Maria, who were carrying a few pounds (over 1.3 kilograms) of diamonds sewn into their clothing, which had given them a degree of protection from the firing. However, they were speared with bayonets as well. Olga sustained a gunshot wound to the head. Maria and Anastasia were said to have crouched up against a wall covering their heads in terror until they were shot. Yurovsky killed Tatiana who died from a single shot to the back of her head. Alexei received two bullets to the head, right behind the ear. While the bodies were being placed on stretchers, one of the girls cried out and covered her face with her arm. One of the killers grabbed a rifle and bayoneted her in the chest, but when it failed to penetrate he pulled out his revolver and shot her in the head. I am sorry if I am taking too long," he said while turning and looking at Jamerson who told him to take as much time as he needed.

"In the aftermath, it was clear to Yurovsky and members of the assassination team, that the children had worn undergarments that had jewelry sown into them thus reflecting the bullets from their weapons. He gave the order to collect all of the loose items from the blood and body waste on the floor and to bring it to his room. He then ordered some members of the killing squad to strip the bodies of their clothing where more jewelry was discovered.

(Slide advance) This is the room where the assassinations took place:

In the aftermath of the 1917 revolution, numerous reports in foreign newspapers had suggested wanton vandalism and the loss of a collection reportedly worth $500 million. Now, over a century after the Romanovs were assassinated by the Bolsheviks, the whereabouts of their jewelry remains an enduring mystery. Which pieces made it out of the Revolution and into Europe intact? Which were pulled apart by the government and sold as stones? Which of the ones sewn into their clothing blunted the Bolsheviks bullets? Where are they all now? This remains a developing story. Catalogues created in 1922, and now the property of USGS library in Virginia, contains images of three pieces—including a sapphire tiara, a sapphire bracelet, and an emerald necklace—that were missing from the 1925 inventory conducted in Moscow. Here is a picture of the missing items," (slide advance). On the screen was a display of the three missing pieces of jewelry.

After taking another sip of water, Vasili Sokalov looked at the crowd before him and continued. "In 1925, upon discovery of the theft of these items, our investigators focused on this man, Alexander Orlov, (slide advance) who worked in the room containing the safe housing the jewelry. Unfortunately, during his interrogation, he was found hanging in his cell.

"Yeah right," Pinheiro thought. "You mean during his torture, he decided suicide was his only escape."

"Over the years, our government continued in our attempt to locate the missing jewelry. Recently, we received information that the jewelry made its way in 1925, to a relative of Anatoly Pavlenko, who lived in St. Petersburg. By the time we got this information however, he had died of old age and neither his wife or former mistress could provide any additional information. In searching his house, we found a note hidden in a book referring to the transfer of Romanoff items to Yakov Yurovskhy for a small sum of money considering what the jewelry was worth. We believe that the missing jewelry items were then stolen by Alexander Orlov, and sold to the father of Anatoly Pavlenko who currently has the Romanoff jewels." With that, he turned to Jamerson and walked back to his seat.

"Thank you, Mr. Sokalov, for your comprehensive review of the stolen gems. The Russian Government has asked for our help in locating and retrieving those items and the involvement of Pavlenko. We have packets for each of you to take back to your agencies in hope that you can use whatever resources you have to further this investigation. As usual, the NSA and other intelligence agencies are available to assist." She looked at staff members located on the west wall and nodded to them. They quickly picked up packets and began distributing them.

Chapter
Two

The flight from San Francisco to Miami International airport was long and exhausting due to their layover in Atlanta. They hailed a cab to the Biltmore Hotel in Coral Gables where two rooms had been reserved. Ismail had already taken some good humor flack when he boarded the plane in San Francisco wearing a Kansas City Chiefs jersey since most of the passengers on their flight were bound for Super Bowl LIV to support their San Francisco 49ers. Jeannie was one of them.

Homeland Security agent Richard Pinheiro had surprised Jeannie with the tickets for the big game once the two teams were announced. It was going to be their first official romantic get-away following the conclusion of the three terrorist acts in the bay area. Fortunately, only one bombing was successful in San Francisco where the crowd of the faithful were killed outside a Russian Orthodox church hosting the pontiff. The second attack at the Cow Palace where the President was holding a fundraiser was prevented by Jeannie and her team as well as a very observant sniper. The third attack was never reported to the public to prevent panic. The terrorists were in the process of blowing up the BART tube connecting San Francisco to Oakland.

"I can't believe I am here," Ismail said. "Look at all the fans."

"Yeah, most of them are Niner fans if you notice," Jeannie replied

"Nah, you need to get your eyes checked boss. Those are Chief jerseys, not 49ers," he said. "Can you believe my cousin, your boyfriend, got these great tickets?"

"Just remember buddy. Ricky got these tickets for him and me. He got called away on a case and I invited you. You are welcome," Jeannie said.

"Boy, does that mean I am indebted to you for the rest of my life?" Ismail asked.

"Absolutely," she replied with a smile on her face.

The tailgaters were in full force in the parking lot outside Hard Rock Stadium. One guy was deep-frying a whole turkey. Another had ribs, chicken, and corn-on-the-cob on his grill. The aroma was out of this world. Each tailgater seemed to be competing with each other but all in good fun.

"Gee, I don't see any Portuguese food," Ismail said, but before Jeannie could respond, one of the cooks yelled, "Hey, over here."

Ismail turned to see a Kansas City Chiefs fan plating up breakfast for Ismail containing scrambled eggs, hash browns, and a link of linguica. "Hey, a fan with good taste both in his team and his food," Ismail said after thanking the cook. "See, you are rooting for the wrong team," he said while taking his first bite. Jeannie just rolled her eyes.

Another cook wearing his Joe Montana jersey near his motorhome, overheard the banter and not to be outdone, handed Jeannie a pulled-pork sandwich and offered her a soda. She said thank you and accepted the sandwich and diet Coke since she did not want to offend him. The sandwich smelled so good, she was glad she accepted.

"Thank you, cousin," Ismail said while taking another bite.

Judge Swartz left his downtown office and was looking forward to getting home in time for the big game. He didn't care which team won. If the Chiefs came out on top, it would be their first Super Bowl win and if the San Francisco 49ers pulled it off, their dynasty was on the rise again. He had chicken wings marinating at home with chips, beer, and nacho cheese as compliments. At halftime he would switch over to homemade submarine sandwiches and his famous chili. He walked to his Audi A6 and noticed that the light over his parked vehicle was out. "I will have to tell maintenance about that on Monday," he thought to himself.

The underground garage smelled of exhaust fumes, motor oil, and rubber. Reaching his car, he placed his briefcase down next to the passenger front door, while reaching into his pocket for the electronic car lock fob.

From the darkness a figure emerged dressed in black from head to toe. The black ski mask only had cutouts for his eyes and mouth. In the figure's right hand was a plastic bag containing a Ruger .22 caliber semi-automatic with suppressor. The bag would catch the expended shell casings. Walking slowly behind the judge's location, without hesitation he fired a round into the back of his skull. The judge was dead before hitting the cold parking lot floor. The figure walked up to the still body and placed the weapon over the judge's heart, firing one additional round. He then left the garage avoiding all overhead cameras. "The Star Chamber court will have one less judge as of today," Joey thought. He removed his gloves but kept the ski mask on for a few minutes after exiting the parking garage just in case there were some other cameras about.

At halftime the two teams were tied 10-10. "Looks like it is going to come down to the wire," Jeannie said as she got up to make a phone call to Pinheiro, use the restroom, and pick up some food.

"Yeah, but the Chiefs will turn it on in the second half, you watch," Ismail said as the person behind him, wearing a Niner's jersey, said, "only if the referrers continue to blow calls."

"Hi, how are the seats?" Pinhiero said immediately after answering the phone.

"They're great but a guy sitting next to me is a pain in the ass," she said while trying to suppress a laugh. Pinheiro laughed. "Is my cousin getting under your skin?" he asked.

"Yeah, because I would rather have you sitting next to me," she responded. "How was your briefing?"

"It wasn't bad. Do you know much about Russian history?" he asked.

"I took a course in it when I was an undergraduate, why?"

"Well the briefing was about the theft of the Romanoff jewelry, you know, the last Czar of Russia and the assassination of his entire family," he said.

"Yes, it was fascinating learning about their civil war and what happened to Czar Nicholas II and his family. Did they talk about Rasputin? That guy had a lot to do with the destruction of the royal monarchy."

"No, I don't remember them talking about Rasputin, but the presenter went into a lot of detail about the assassinations and the fact that the bullets of the assassins could not penetrate the undergarments of the Czar's daughters."

"Yeah, what a tragic time. After the assassins killed the royal family and a few of their servants if I remember correctly, they loaded the victims into trucks and then threw them down some mine shafts or wells. They poured acid on the bodies but were upset with the results so they dragged them back up and burnt. Why were you given a short history of the Russian Revolution?" Jeannie asked.

"There are three pieces of the Romanoff jewelry worth millions stolen back in 1925. The Russian government, aka the FSB, are fingering Anatoly Pavlenko as having possession of the stolen property."

"That asshole. Yeah, I can see him being involved with stolen Romanoff jewelry. We both know he is into anything and everything to fund Antifa and any other radical left-wing groups. He's probably using the gems as collateral or something. Shit, his house in Pacific Heights is on the market for $34 million dollars. His wealth came from his father who some believed played both sides between the Nazis and the Russians during World War II. I would love to see him take the fall. Hell, he's in his late eighties or early nineties so a prison term would equal the death penalty. So, the briefing was to track down the missing gems and tie it to him?"

"Something like that. I am not sure how the DHS fits in except possibly having a chance to connect him with Antifa or the other groups he funds – maybe get him on a RICA violation or conspiracy. I am taking the packet they gave me back to the department and run it up the flag pole and see what the higher-ups want to do with it. You two are flying back tonight or tomorrow?" he asked.

"We changed our flight from the one you got us to an upgrade of a direct flight to San Fran. We will leave early tomorrow morning, but with the jet lag, I won't go into the office until the next day. God, I miss you," Jeannie said.

"I miss you a whole bunch too. Better get back to the game and tell that person sitting next to you that if he messes with you, I will kick his ass."

"Will do," Jeannie said while blowing a kiss into the phone for Pinheiro. "Love you."

"Love you too," Pinheiro said as they both hung up their cells.

Chapter Three

The number one threat to the United States is the lone wolf jihadist. They are the hardest to track and hide in the shadows – in cyberspace, on extremist websites, where al Qaeda and ISIS try to recruit them. To hunt them down the NSA and FBI have to be online since this is where most of the radicalization of future jihadists occurs.

On February 4, 2020, at an undisclosed location, FBI counter-intelligence analyst Peggy Jacobs notified her JTTF (Joint Terrorism Task Force) supervisor Ruth Billingham to look at her computer screen.

"I found this unanimous post from a user calling himself Zaid Abu Sayyaf. What caught my eye are these last two postings: (1) he is already in the United States and (2) he wants to attack the United States and serve as a soldier of al Qaeda as soon as possible."

Jacob's supervisor asked her if she had been able to pull up the source. "Yes," Jacobs said, "looks like he's in Waco, Texas. He is signaling to other individuals to see if they can help him secure the "tools", guns and explosives, he needs for a planned attack. He yearns for action."

"Great, Waco again. Hope it doesn't turn into another Branch Davidian shootout," said Billingham who reached for a phone on Jacob's desk. "Get me our Dallas field office," she said while looking at Jacob. "It is going to be critical for them to find out who he is and his exact location. They can do a more in-depth analysis to see if he is a real threat."

On February 5th at the FBI field office in Dallas, Agent Paul Wilson, acting on the information received from Billingham, tracked the IP address to a 21-year old Jordanian named Omar Hassan. He pulled up a passport photo and began a more intensive background into the possible radicalized individual. He then went into the larger briefing room at the Dallas office and placed the photograph of Hassan in the upper center of a white-board. He printed Hassan's full name under the photo with an aka of Zaid Abu Sayyaf. He then drew a line to the right where he taped a photo of Hassan's father. Below Hassan was a Google overhead photo showing their residence in the outskirts of Waco. The three-bedroom non-descript home had no neighbors. It was pretty much isolated from other homes.

By eleven o'clock that morning, six additional agents arrived in the briefing room. SAC Dani Shapiro was the last to arrive. She had been the SAC at the Dallas field office for over a year and had won the support of all of her staff as a hard, but fair supervisor. Unless you did something outstanding beyond your normal duties, you did not receive praise from her. Because of that, when you did, it meant something.

"What do we have?" she asked as she took a seat.

Wilson turned to the group after placing some other documents on the white-board. "Ok, said Agent Wilson, "the JTTF found postings on one of the jihadists websites by this man using the username Zaid Abu Sayyaf. His real name as you can see, is Omar Hassan, a 21-year old Jordanian who came to the United States about two years ago with his father." Wilson pointed to Hassan's father. "Hassan's postings are becoming more and more threatening and he is trying to link up with someone who can provide him with bomb-making material and the knowledge of how to become a soldier of al Qaeda. JTTF stated that his postings appear to be "real" and not just some boasting on his part. He idolizes the dead Osama bin Laden and wants help to pull off his attacks, plural. It appears that his posting using his IP address is coming from this residence outside of Waco. After reviewing the postings forwarded to us from JTTF, it appears he may be the real deal."

"Thanks Paul. Nice job on the workup. Ok, we need to put eyes on Hassan and track his every movement," said Shapiro. "Paul come up with how much manpower you and the rest of your team will need to track him and to set up a tactical surveillance of his residence. Jesus, he lives in no-mans-land and will be hard to track. Everyone out there probably knows everyone else. Ok people, I am making this a priority one investigation."

Agent James Robinson and four other agents began tracking Hassan. His normal travels took him from his home to a fast-food restaurant just inside the city limits of Waco along the I35 corridor. On the third day of tracking Hassan, Robinson decided to enter the restaurant and observe Hassan up close. He waited 15-minutes after Hassan entered the eatery before entering. Fortunately, Hassan was working at the cash register taking customer orders.

"Can I take your order?" he said when it was Robinson's turn. "Yes, I would like a burger, order of fries, and a diet Coke," came the reply.

"Will this be for here?" asked Hassan.

"Yes, please."

"Would you like medium or large fries?" Hassan asked.

"Regular would be fine," Robinson said waiting to find out how much to pay. He then found a table that would allow him to observe and hear Hassan interact with customers while waiting for his food. He ate while watching Hassan for almost a half-hour. Hassan was only 5'7" and thin sporting what appeared to be three to four days growth of facial hair. Robinson felt that Hassan appeared to be a gregarious outgoing young Arab man who could easily pass for a college student, but very unremarkable in any other respect. He did a good job of keeping the monster inside.

The agents were correct. Trailing Hassan was not easy. Living out in rural Texas with few people on the road forced another increase in surveillance teams. When not at work, Hassan was back online pleading for assistance in his jihad quest. Fearing that he might link up with another terrorist cell, whether it be al Qaeda or ISIS, SAC Shapiro ordered an undercover Arab agent to attempt contact via the Web with Hassan to see if he was the real deal. To understand him and his motivations, they decided to engage him in conversation.

The legal department at the Dallas field office informed the agents that they did not have enough to make a case against Hassan at this time. His defense would be that he was only exercising his 1st Amendment rights since no one had actually seen him typing his postings.

Chapter Four

Seeing Jeannie returning to her seat with hands and arms cradling hot dogs and two beers, Ismail said, "What no nachos?" "You're lucky you're getting this wearing that Chiefs jersey," Jeannie responded. "Good girl," said a lady wearing a 49ers jersey sitting behind her.

The half-time show started and although Ismail liked the costumes being worn by the two star performers and hoped for a wardrobe malfunction, he told Jeannie that he hoped his wife had the younger Flores children leave the room. "Gee, they call this empowering woman?" Jeannie asked Ismail. Ismail agreed that pole dancing was something that should stay in a strip club, not at a half-time show.

By the end of the 3rd quarter, the Niners were ahead 20-10 over Ismail's Chiefs which encouraged Jeannie to keep up harassing him. "Still one quarter left," he would reply. Sure enough, the Niners took their foot off the accelerator and allowed the Chiefs to win the game. "Oh well, they had a great season," Jeannie said to the lady behind her. "Yeah, it sure looked to me that the referees were for Kansas Chief with all the blown calls.

Looking at Ismail who could hardly contain his smile, Jeannie told him to not say a word if he wants to fly home tomorrow since she had the flight tickets. Ismail just bowed his head in silence while bump fisting another Chief's fan next to him.

After ringing the doorbell, a butler answered the massive front door of the mansion owned by Anatoly Pavlenko and invited the sergeant-of-arms of the SDL (Sons and Daughters of Liberty) to enter. He kept mental note of the number of security personnel he could observe both outside and inside the estate. Pavlenko bought the original house three years ago and had it leveled to the ground. Then he painstakingly found an architect that promised to design a residence with thought, care, and purpose of maximizing inspiration, ease of living, and connection with the city and bay. The current house replaced the single-story former house with a five-story architectural marvel. It was beyond doubt the most technologically advanced residence in San Francisco. It was environmentally designed to enhance residents' physical, mental, and emotional health. The four-bedroom, three-and-a-half baths home located in

Pacific Heights combined sophisticated luxury with leading-edge health and wellness. The garden level of the home led to a private oasis. Stunning views atop the roof deck spanned from the Golden Gate to Alcatraz. Its interior had a technology-enabled platform for sustainable living, with custom finishes for modern tastes. The home was a vision for what an elevated living environment can be, especially for someone as wealthy as Pavlenko.

As he was being escorted through the residence, he paid particular attention to the layout of the interior of the home as he had done with the exterior design details. Besides the home's modern façade, he noticed a secured entryway with a gas-lit pathway to the front door. The driveway had a secure entryway for three cars. It had a Siedal biometric keypad. There were two terraces, one facing north and the other south. The roof deck had sweeping bay views and a fire-pit culminating with a privacy-scaped outdoor entertainment area with a large spa and television set.

All of the bedrooms were located on the top floor, each having a private entrance exterior roof terrace. Pavelenko was found sitting in his study behind a huge carved cherry wood desk. On the top of the desk were three gorgeous jewelry items on display being admired by Pavelenko when the former SDL leader entered. "Joseph, how good to see you," Pavelenko said without rising from his seat. "Sit, sit, would you like something to drink? Coffee, soda, water?"

"No thank you. And what do you have here?" he asked.

"Ah, these are the most beautiful jewelry items of the Romanoff dynasty. Do you know much about Russian history?" Pavelenko asked.

"No, nothing really," came the reply.

"Sad that your American schools do not spend time anymore teaching European history. I don't think they teach American history either. Am I correct?" Not waiting for an answer, he continued looking at each item with a magnifying glass. "During the Russian Revolution, the Bolsheviks decided that the former Czar, Czar Nicholas II, and his family, had to be assassinated. After the deed was done, all of the former monarchs' jewelry was confiscated by the new regime.

"Must be worth a ton," the SDL leader said.

"I have received estimates between $700 million to $1 billion, but who knows."

"How did you get it? I am sure the Russians had no intention of selling such items."

Laughing, Pavelenko put down the magnifying glass and said, "No, I can assure you that the former Soviet Union, and now the Russian government would never sell such items. There are many other pieces, some even more valuable than these, but I was able to secure these. Ah, but you asked how I got them, didn't you? My father obtained them from a source inside Cheka. Have you heard this name, Cheka?

"No, as I said, I know nothing about Russian history."

"The Cheka was the secret police of the former Soviet Union in 1925. Their name has changed over the years from Cheka to KGB to now, the FSB, but that is not important. My father became friends with one of the Cheka agents and offered him money to steal these items. After my father died, they became mine."

"What happened to the Cheka agent that stole the items? I am sure the secret police did an investigation."

While waving his hand as if it was a trivial matter, Pavlenko said, "He killed himself while being interrogated. The Cheka were a blood-thirsty group I can tell you. But, by the time their investigation focused on him, these items were on their way to Germany and later here in the United States. Would you like to look at them more closely?"

While walking around the desk to get a closer look at the items, he made note of the safe model mounted into the wall of the study. He easily recognized the V-Line Quick Vault Locking safe and was familiar with its features. Not only was it made of a durable metal that makes it safe for a person to store items within the unit, but it is also drill and torch resistant and bulletproof. This prevented people from being able to access it by trying to shoot their way through the safe. There is one adjustable shelf allowing the owner to quickly and easily organize their items such as the Romanoff jewelry. Plus, the shelf is removable if a person desires to not use it at all. He loved the design of the safe, since it was made so that the door was indented and flushed with the wall. This ensures that the owner could easily disguise it behind a painting or other hanging object without it being noticeable.

The safe locks had a mechanical locking system that included an additional backup key. The push-button system allowed a person to create a unique code that they can enter to gain access into the safe. However, should the owner have a situation where they forgot the code or where they need to allow someone else to gain access, there is a backup key that comes along with the safe. The safe is designed to be pry-resistant. No one would be able to dislodge the door or pull the safe apart using a crowbar or other similar object. The hinges had been turned to the inside which makes it nearly impossible for anyone to be able to tear the door off. It is a fantastically designed safe he thought, but he knew of a way to gain access when the time came.

"You like, dah?" Pavelenko asked pointing at the gems.

"Yes, very nice," came the response while walking back to his side of the desk. "I am here because I need more funding for the event in Berkeley next week."

"The event on the University of California campus?" Pavelenko asked. "The one where the conservative talk show host will be present?"

"Yes, Megan Thompson. She is a rising star in the conservative talk show world and could command a large audience which we hope to stop. I want to organize a group of forty Antifa members to mix in with the crowd both outside and inside the auditorium. I think that $20 per hour should attract enough bodies for the job."

"I am familiar with Ms. Thompson. Too bad, for an attractive intelligent woman she does not understand the need for globalism." He opened a drawer in his desk and removed a metal box much smaller than the box that must have contained the Romanoff jewelry. After opening it, he pulled out a large bundle of $20 bills. He split the bundle in half and without counting, handed it to the former SDL leader. He then looked up and asked if the murder of Swartz was his handy work. He did not get a reply, only a smile as the SDL leader left the study again paying close attention to his surroundings.

Chapter
Five

Returning to his safe house in Oakland, Joey
Rogers, 31 years old, sporting a shaved head
and Fu Manchu mustache, went into the
kitchen where he found the rest of his cohorts. Sitting
at the kitchen table were Amy Perry, a 24-years old
college graduate. former part-time model and Joey's
girlfriend. Next to her was Billy Armstrong, 31 years
old former cellmate of Joey, both having served time
in Folsom State Prison for armed robbery. Billy had
long almost black hair that reached the small of his
back, now in a ponytail. Joey did not think of himself
as a mere assassin. He preferred to be looked upon as a
coordinator – a leader of specialists, who himself was
the most cold-blooded of them all.

"We will get some food after I tell you our plans for
next week at Berkeley and what I saw at Pavelenko's
mansion today," said Joey.

"The motherfucker actually let you in his pad?" asked Vicki Sanders, the most radical member of the group. She was what some called a professional student, never having a job, but lived and breathed on university campuses, chat rooms, or book stores on Telegraph Avenue. Anti-American, pro-Socialist, and a love for anarchy, she was the spark plug of the group but constantly had to be controlled by Joey. She was the oldest member of the group at 47-years- old. She still dressed like a hippy from the 1960s but now streaked her long brown hair with either, blue, green, or yellow highlights – sometimes, all three. She never failed to have a bitch about the U.S. government and was no fan of the sitting President.

"What was it like inside?" came the next question before Joey could answer. It came from Sandi Hayes, the lesbian lover of Sanders. Only 18-years-old and joining the group probably to punish her wealthy parents, she was the baby of the group taking all of her leads from Sanders. Before answering their questions, Joey asked where Chico was at?"

Chico Hernandez, a slightly obese 42-year-old Mexican-American finally arrived completing the group. Also, an ex-con, Hernandez did time for a string of armed car robberies in the Los Angeles area. He was able to get some of the charges dropped and copped to a plea bargain giving him 10 years in prison which resulted in him only doing 3 ½. "Hey, we didn't have anything to eat so I went and picked some up," he said, carrying several large bags and a cup carrier with food and sodas coming from a nearby In-and-Out Burger place. "Anyone hungry?" he asked while putting the items down on the table. "Hell yes," said Billy who helped himself to the closest bag of goodies.

Joey continued to fill them in about his visit with Pavelenko and the safe and jewelry he had seen. He did not feel the need to show them the large amount of cash he had in his rear pocket since it was to be used mostly for recruitment for the event at UC.

"We are encouraged by your enthusiasm," typed the undercover Arab FBI agent from the secured computer lab inside the Dallas Field Office to Hassan. The Dallas FBI team wanted to see how far Hassan was ready to go. There was a need to assess him quickly before he decided to enlist with al Qaeda or ISIS. The last thing the FBI wanted was Hassan hooking up with them.

"We are convinced that you have the talent necessary to be a soldier of al Qaeda. We are the only organization that can provide you with the tools and guidance for your jihad."

Hassan's lack of immediate response was nerve-racking, but it gave the Dallas team time to dig up everything they could on him. He was born in Aljoun, Jordan. Initially he was close to his father but that disintegrated when his father divorced his mother. After the divorce, his father took Hassan to

Texas leaving behind his friends and relatives. Their relationship was tenuous as best but went downhill quickly after his mother died back in Jordan. At that point their relationship turned negative and there appears to have been an uptick in his visits to known jihadist websites.

While working her way through her stack of phone messages Jeannie heard a knock on her door. She looked up and saw SAC Lomax standing there. "How was the Super Bowl?" he asked. After Jeannie responded, he asked if she had time for a cup of coffee. She followed him to the breakroom on their floor. They both took a seat across from each other.

"There is going to be another major shake-up in the bureau next week. The President will appoint a new Attorney General and then heads will roll. The liberals will bitch and complain but the President will be in his right to hire and fire whomever he wishes. It appears by all reliable sources, that he will win re-election in a landslide and so he is about to flex his wings, not showing a bit of concern over the scam impeachment crap." He handed Jeannie a folded note listing several agents names assigned to their bureau. "These individuals will be notified this Friday of their terminations at the close of business. Keep this confidential."

Jeannie looked at the names, knowing all of them. She was never impressed with their work ethic, production, or their professionalism. "This will reduce our manpower until we get replacements," Jeannie said.

"Yes, but I have been assured by Washington that replacements will be here by mid-week so barring any major events, we should be ok," he responded. Lomax's cellphone vibrated in his suit pocket. He pulled it out and saw Jamerson and a D.C., phone number on his display. "Huh, do you know anyone in D.C. with the last name Jamerson?" he asked.

"Doesn't ring a bell," she replied.

"Well, I better call back and see what this Jamerson wants," he said as he rose and headed to the hallway leading to his office. Jeannie filled her coffee cup and was preparing to leave the breakroom when Darcy walked in.

"Hi Jeannie, how was the big game?" she asked

"It was awesome. I know I lost a lot of what was shown on television, but the energy of over 68,000 people in a stadium rooting for their respective team was unbelievable. Of course, starting tonight, I will watch the game again since I recorded it to see what I missed."

"Maybe not," said Lomax who had returned to the breakroom. "I called Jamerson back and I need to see the two of you in my office," as he waved a piece of notepaper in his left hand. "Find Flores and get him here also." With that he turned and walked back to his office.

Chapter Six

Agent Wilson finished addressing the task force at the Dallas field office by saying that it appears Hassan is in the "jihad cool stage." He loved what he was seeing on television and the Internet showing American soldiers being killed by al Qaeda and ISIS and cannot wait to become one of their foot soldiers. He had his father, his new home, and especially his new country. He had rejected the non-violent tenants of his religion and adopted the violent path of al Qaeda. He was ripe for radicalization. He was ready to carry out a violent act.

Finally, after weeks, Hassan responded to the undercover agents' postings. The agents' carefully worded emails had attracted Hassan. He had found a person who could fulfill his dream of becoming a soldier of al Qaeda. He believed that he had contacted an al Qaeda cell. The undercover agent made Hassan believe that he was a lieutenant in the terrorist organization and had worked closely with the former Osama bin Laden.

"If you are with me, I want to meet you, learn from you. But if you are American intelligence, you can go to hell," Hassan posted. Fearing that they might lose Hassan, more and more emails were sent to him. Hassan continued to communicate thinking it truly was an al Qaeda sleeper cell. A bonding had taken place and Hassan expressed even more possible sites and his devotion to al Qaeda.

Still lacking hard evidence to make an arrest, the Dallas team needed to keep constant communication with Hassan until he made his move. Time was of the essence since he talked about the need to get handguns and high capacity clips. The task force worried that Hassan may become frustrated and carry out a lone wolf attack on a church, cinema, mall, or even at this workplace.

There was also the possibility that Hassan was playing the FBI for fools. His emails contained more and more calls for jihad but the FBI had to avoid even suggesting acts of violence. It had to formulate in Hassan's mind alone to avoid entrapment. Hassan had to fully layout his plans. He could not be perceived by a court as having been manufactured by the FBI. To avoid this, several communications took place in which the agent tried to talk Hassan out of committing a violent act. Each time Hassan became agitated and displayed anger with the undercover agent. He was vehement in his desire to carry out an act of jihad. He wanted to kill or cut the throats of Americans. Because of the increased violent rhetoric, Agent Wilson decided it was time to meet face-to-face with Hassan.

Hassan was sent an email telling him that there was a sergeant of al Qaeda here in the United States who would arrive in Dallas to meet with him. This would require a 1 ½ hour drive by Hassan from Waco. This, Agent Wilson felt, would show the court later, that Hassan had plenty of time to back off his request for violence. Hassan did not back off but became excited over the future meeting. The undercover agent who had talked with Hassan the last few weeks, would pose as the sergeant.

A Four Seasons Hotel in Dallas was selected for the meeting. The parking lot would allow for agents to monitor the arrival and departure of Hassan and many of the suites had adjacent rooms with a pass-door that the agents could use in case something went wrong. Two days before the meet, agents placed cameras and audio bugs in the meeting room. In the next room they placed the monitoring and recording equipment.

On the morning of the meet, Hassan was seen leaving his home and stopping at a nearby gas station. He went in to pay for his gas and returned to his vehicle carrying something to eat and drink. The ninety-five-mile drive would be hot since his car's air condition did not work. He stopped twice on the way to Dallas. The time he spent inside the two fast-food restaurants was probably for a bathroom break and to stretch his legs the surveillance team surmised.

About two hours later, Agent Wilson and the task force heard surveillance team one announced that Hassan had just driven into the parking lot of the hotel. Even with the stops, he had made good time. He parked his car and walked quickly to the hotel entrance. "He is all yours, surveillance team one out." Wilson acknowledged the transmission and told the team to get ready. "It's showtime," he said.

An agent in the hotel lobby said that Hassan had just entered the elevator and was headed up to the room. The monitoring and recording equipment was started, while the undercover agent waited for the knock on the suite's door which came a short time later. Greetings in Arabic were shared, and the undercover agent motioned to the table where he had been sitting. There was no weapon visible. It was now a make or break moment with the stake of thousands of Americans at stake. The ticking time-bomb thinking he was meeting with an al Qaeda sergeant was being recorded a few feet away.

Hassan was very confident and showed no fear. He displayed no nervousness, only a coldness and eagerness to listen to the al Qaeda representative. Their conversation continued in Arabic, so Wilson and the other task force team members were forced to bend over another Arabi FBI agent's shoulder who was typing on his computer, a translation in English, of what was being said. This and the agent's body language was the only way for Wilson to interpret what was transpiring. Looks and glances were shared between the translator and Wilson. The translator, after only a few minutes, looked at Wilson and motioned that this was a true believer and jihadist next door.

Hassan told the undercover agent that he had visited several buildings in Dallas and wanted to bring down a building like bin Laden did in New York. To do so however, he needed a large bomb. He did not have the resources or material to get one alone. The undercover agent said that he would relay Hassan's wishes to the new al Qaeda leader and set up a second meet the following week when Hassan was not working.

Hassan left satisfied that he had connected with a sleeper cell of al Qaeda that would make his dream come true of becoming not only a soldier of the infamous terrorist group, but a person who would also bring a building of America to the ground taking American lives in the process.

The lobby agent clicked his mic alerting the mobile surveillance team that Hassan was about to leave the hotel. Agent Wilson opened the pass-through door and walked up to the standing undercover agent. "What do you think?" he asked. "Paul, I just looked into the eyes of Satan. This guy is going all the way. He is the real deal," came the answer.

The next day online communication resumed. Wilson also briefed SAC Shapiro of the meeting. "We need to keep a tight net around this asshole," she said. "Use all the resources you need. What about legal? Do we have enough to pick him up?"

"Not yet. They feel we still need more for an arrest, but they did give me the go-ahead to secure a search warrant."

"Won't that tip him off?" asked Shapiro.

"Not if you concur on how I would like to do this," he said. "My thought is that we hit the house when both Hassan and his father are absent. We don't take anything except to copy Hassan's computer hard drive. We leave no traces of us even being there. If we glean anything that can be used to get an arrest warrant, so be it, but if not, we can see what else he has on his computer."

"If legal signs off on it, go for it. Keep me in the loop," Shapiro said while returning to her office.

The following day after the search warrant was obtained, the surveillance teams followed both Hassan and his father away from the residence. Once Hassan was at work as well as his father, Wilson and two other agents hit the house. Fortunately, a bedroom window belonging to Hassan's father was found open. An agent climbed in and then opened the front door.

The house was decorated Spartan style with a used couch in the front room across from an off-brand flat-screen television. The house smelled of Arabic spices. The single bathroom needed a deep cleaning. Nothing of evidentiary value was found in any part of the house until the agents entered Hassan's room. The room had been set up as a shrine to the dead al Qaeda leader Osama bin Laden. Pictures of the dead terrorist's decorated every wall in the room. One showed bin Laden, dressed in white, firing an AK-47.

The search warrant allowed for the uploading of Hassan's computer contents onto a thumb drive to be analyzed later. After 45-minutes, the search was concluded, and the agents left without leaving a trace of their being present.

The next two days, panic took over the task force team. Several emails had been sent to Hassan but he had not returned any correspondence. Wilson checked in with the surveillance team who early that morning tracked Hassan to his workplace. "Is his car still there?" asked Wilson. "Affirm," came the response. "Ok, do me a favor. One of you two needs to go into the hamburger joint and put eyes on him. Order a burger and so on." "Roger that. We were getting hungry anyway."

Wilson glanced at his watch: 1:35 in the afternoon. Hassan normally is at work until 3:30. "Team leader, we have a problem."

Chapter Seven

I smail entered Lomax's office without knocking since he saw Jeannie and Darcy already sitting in the room. "Flores, I am glad you are here. I just got started filling in these two (motioning to Jeannie and Darcy) about my phone call with Agent Jamerson of the NSA. There were no other chairs in Lomax's office so Ismail stood next to the seated Darcy. Our Dallas field office had been tracking a lone wolf terrorist named Omar Hassan. Darcy can give you the particular later. They have concluded that he has been radicalized and on the verge of committing an act of terrorism using a bomb."

"So how do we fit in?" asked Ismail.

"They lost him," Jeannie said.

"What?" asked Ismail.

"After months of tailing this guy with the tightest 24/7 net they could use in such a small town, he gave the surveillance team the slip from where he works," Lomax said. "They checked with his father and co-workers, but no one knows where he might be. The thought is that either Hassan or someone he works with, spotted the surveillance teams and he spooked. For the last month, he has not been on the Internet until last night. His IP address popped up here in San Francisco and he is once again talking to one of our undercover agents. He said that he thought American intelligence was monitoring him, so he got out quickly. He has spent the last few weeks scouting new sites in our city for jihad and wants the person he believed was part of an al Qaeda cell that he met in Dallas, to meet with him here so he can carry out his plan." Lomax stopped talking and looked at the three agents before him.

"Jeannie, have you spoken recently with Pinheiro?" Lomax asked.

"No sir. I tried calling him a few times in the last several hours, but it always goes to voice mail," came her response.

"It's probably because he is on a plane as I speak. Jamerson alerted the DHS and Pinheiro is flying out here with the undercover agent from Dallas that previously met with Hassan." Jeannie felt excited about seeing Ricky and the time that they will be able to spend with each other. She also felt that she was blushing since she had plans for her Rickey when he arrived - unexpected surprise to say the least.

"Darcy, I need you to connect with Jamerson or whoever she feels you need to work with from the

NSA. We need to track down the location of his IP address. She said it was around San Francisco, but shit, that could mean South San Fran, Burlingame, Marin, Daly City, Pacifica, just to name a few. Get Burk and have him gather all the intel the NSA and our Dallas field office has asap. I want everything they have on their walls up in our briefing room. Have him get everything in place before Pinheiro and the Dallas agent gets here. Jeannie, you arrange for the pickup at the airport. I am not sure of the flight number, arrival time, and so on. Ismail, once Darcy tracks down the location of the IP address, do a quick drive by and see what type of place this guy is living in. Wait a minute," Lomas said before starting up again. "This guy might have spotted a bureau car used in his surveillance and he has already been spooked. Maybe Jeannie will loan you her Corvette for the cruise by."

"Sounds great to me," Ismail said as he placed his opened hand in front of Jeannie with a big smile on his face. "Maybe I should change into my Kansas City Chiefs jersey to complete the charade." Jeannie rolled her eyes and fished her car keys out of her front pocket. "Ok, get to work people," said Lomax as Jeannie and Darcy stood following Ismail out of the office.

Joey set up shop at a local Starbucks near the main UC campus. He had scheduled in 15-minute intervals, meetings with individuals who had called saying they were interested in his posts on campus where he offered a $20 per hour activists' job. How long does it take to convince a bunch of idiots to act out for media groups for that amount of money and a promise that they would be provided legal assistance if they got arrested, he thought? Sometimes Joey even offers a bonus if they get arrested. It wasn't his money anyway, it was that fat fuck Russian living in that mansion with the stolen jewelry. All but one person excitedly took the job offer. They were to meet outside a coffee shop on Telegraph Avenue at 6:30 p.m. on Tuesday for final instructions before marching onto the campus shouting and assaulting anyone they felt like hitting. He encouraged them to wear masks or scarfs to protect their identity as well as bats and clubs. Political signs would be provided to them at the coffee shop.

He then returned to their hideout and found Amy waiting for him. "How did it go?" she asked. "Good. I think we have a lot of violent dumbasses that will create havoc tomorrow night." He grabbed her waist and pulled her towards him. "Anyone else in the house?" he asked. "Not that I know of," Amy replied. Joey slid his hands under the white t-shirt she was wearing and found that she did not have a bra on. "Then, let's not lose the opportunity," Joey said as he led her to their bedroom.

That evening everyone was present in the front room. Joey told the group about the event scheduled the following evening and then broached a new subject. "We need cash and I have two ideas on how we might score some." No one spoke and a few leaned forward in interest. "First, I think Anatoly Pavlenko is ready to be taken down. We just need a little more intelligence regarding his security staff, their number, their arrival, departure, routine, and so on. Chico, I want you, Billy, Sandi, and Vicki to stake out the place from a distance for the next week. Do it in shifts so we can determine when his guards show up, when they leave and Pavlenko's schedule if the prick keeps one. Once I am satisfied that we can hit the house successfully, we will make our assault."

"You said you had two ideas," Amy said. "Yes, the second one will be a little more complicated but will take some of the heat off of us while we continue to kill off judges of the Star Chamber. Remember, we are avenging our comrades, the three whom the Star Chamber decided to eliminate as they erased their tracks from discovery. Our comrades did not betray them. They betrayed us." He realized he was shouting and stopped, then returned to the second idea he had.

"Everyone knows Howard Sadler correct?" he asked. "Sure, he's that wealthy son-of-a-bitch that started up the telecommunication business down in Silicon Valley, right?" said Vicki. "He is worth north of $1 billion. He makes his money by having sweatshops around the world make parts for his products and then sells them here and abroad for a ton."

"How are we going to rob him?" asked Hernandez. Everyone turned towards Joey waiting for his answer.

"We are not going to rob him. We are going to kidnap his teenage daughter and hold her for ransom. While I was in Berkeley today recruiting anarchists for the Megan Thompson show, I thought of a way to make some money as well as drive the cops crazy. How many of you know anything about the kidnapping of Patty Hearst?"

Sandi, Armando, and Amy looked clueless, but Vicki quickly answered his question. "Yeah, Patty Hearst and the SLA – the Symbionese Liberation Army, right?" Joey nodded his head telling her to go on. "In 1974, Patty Hearst was shacking with her boyfriend Steven Weed in an apartment just off the Berkeley campus. The SLA was a group of I think 4-6 individuals who shared an ideology and hatred for the rich with their ex-con leader named Cinque. They came up with a plan to snatch Patty from her apartment and hold her for ransom. But they did not ask for money. They made Patty's rich parents deliver free food to different locations in the bay area. After a while, they were able to brainwash Patty into joining their group." Vicki looked at Joey and could see by his facial expression that he was satisfied with her answer.

"So, what? Are we going to kidnap her and make her parents give away free stuff?" asked Chico.

"No, fuck the free stuff crap. Let Bernie Sanders offer that free shit to society. No, instead, we will ask for the money," Joey said looking at the group.

Chapter Eight

Jeannie got up at 6 a.m. and before showering, gave herself a once-over after taking off her clothes. Looks like the gym is paying off, she thought. She saw a few crow's-feet that edged a widened eye. She had accepted the merciless encroachment of age and was keeping her youthful-looking face and her body and had yet to see an ounce of fat. In her view and hopefully that of Ricky, she still looked vibrant and alive as when she graduated from the FBI Academy. While driving to the airport, Jeannie listened to KSFO, the only conservative talk radio show emanating from San Francisco. The two talk show hosts were describing how outrageous the Antifa crowd acted against innocent bystanders who waited in line to see conservative Megan Thompson speak on the University of California, Berkeley campus yesterday. Twenty-nine were seriously injured and one elderly lady died of a heart attack presumably brought on due to the violence she saw. Once she arrived at the bureau, she spent the rest of the morning and afternoon, making sure everything was in place for Ricky and Amir. She also touched bases with the SAC to keep him up to speed.

Jeannie picked up Rickey and the Dallas agent from the airport arrival area in the early evening. Pinheiro introduced Amir Ramzi to Jeannie while placing both his and Ramzi's luggage in the back of the bureau's car trunk. Pinheiro climbed into the front seat of the car, not giving Ramzi the opportunity. "Hello agent Loomis. How have you been?" Pinheiro asked as he winked at Jeannie with his right eye so Ramzi could not see it.

"Fine. It's been a little while," she said will returning his wink. "You two are staying at the Hyatt Regency in Union Square right?" she asked. "Yes, one thing about the DHS, they rarely put us up on a two-star hotel."

"Amir, I guess we in the FBI cannot say that huh?" Jeannie asked.

"No, I can say I have spent many nights in crappy motels where you fight with cockroaches to see who got most of the bed," he replied in perfect English with no hint of a dialect.

"God, your English is phenomenal," Jeannie said, looking back at Amir in the rearview mirror while Pinheiro slyly rubbed the thigh of Jeannie's right leg sending chills up her back and causing her to skip a breath. "Thank you," Amir said. "My parents brought me to the States when I was only 2-years old. We spoke both English and Arabic in our home so I am lucky to speak without the typical Arab accent when speaking with native Americans."

The rest of the drive to the Hyatt was a rehash from Jeannie as to what Lomax had told them about Hassan and the work she and her team had already completed while they were in the air. "His IP address was tracked down to a rundown three-story apartment complex in the Haight.

"I am not familiar with the Haight. What is it?" Amir asked from the backseat as Ricky became more brazen with his hand movements on Jeannie's thigh. "It is the name of a part of the city. Its full name is Haight Ashberry, home of the Hippie Movement in the 1960s. During that time every dropout and runaway in the country fled to the Haight for drugs, free sex or to just drop out. Even old Charlie Manson hung out there for a little while. Other than the rent becoming almost astronomical, the area still attracts rejects," Jeannie said.

"And now jihadist," Amir replied. "And now jihadist," Jeannie said in agreement.

"Here we are gentleman," Jeannie said as a concierge approached their car. She waved him off as Amir and Pinheiro exited the vehicle. "Amir, why don't you go in and get settled. I want to meet with Jeannie's SAC for a few minutes at the bureau. Go ahead and order room service and charge it to my room since everything is under my name. I will catch up with you tomorrow morning for breakfast, say 8 a.m.? "That sounds good to me. See you both tomorrow morning." If Amir suspected anything more than two colleagues talking about work, he did not show it.

After saying that, Amir grabbed his bag and headed into the hotel. "That was smooth," Jeannie said as Pinheiro re-entered the bureau car. Pinheiro looked at the entrance to the hotel and did not see Amir. He then leaned into Jeannie and gave her a long passionate kiss. "Did you really want to see my SAC? He has probably already left for home," Jeannie asked.

"No, what I want to see is the inside of your bedroom," Ricky said giving her another kiss.

"So you think we can knock off Pavlenko house?" Amy asked Joey. "It is so huge, and Vicki said that she and Sandi counted four security officers each shift."

"Yes, with the information the four of them gathered this last week, I think I have a plan that I will share with everyone tonight. Here, handing her a $100 bill. Go pick up 3-4 pizzas and drinks and I will fill everyone in at dinner."

Having completed their last shift of watching Pavlenko's house, Vicki and Sandi, with the help of Chico, approached the backyard of Judge Wayne Katamoto. Chico, being the tallest of the three, easily looked over the fence and found the Judge laying in a lounge chair asleep next to his koi pond and waterfall. Katamoto, after retiring from the bench two years ago, still quenched his thirst of applying justice with his involvement with the Star Chamber. Meeting in secret, the court tried defendants in absentia who felt that due to their political or celebrity status, were above the law. Recently, the court had to suspend their proceedings indefinitely due to circumstances involving the arrest of Judge Baldwin, a Star Chamber judge, for child pornography. With law enforcement converging on the court, the court went dark.

Chico reached over the fence and released the locking mechanism. He then allowed Vicki and Sandi to enter with him following. Sandi was amazed at the crystal-clear water of the koi pond, the soothing sound of the waterfall, and the beautiful fish swimming on the surface. Although for most people a bee sting is painful but otherwise relatively harmless, in people like Judge Katamoto with insect sting allergies, stings can trigger a dangerous anaphylactic reaction that is potentially deadly, especially if the injection were to contain one-hundred times the normal amount of venom, which is normally between 5 and 50 micrograms of fluid.

Vicki pulled out a syringe from a pouch she wore as a purse around her waist. She shook the syringe and noticed a slight air bubble in the solution. Shit, she thought, that will be the least of his problem. With

Chico now standing in front of Katamoto and Sandi behind the judge's head, Chico jumped and came crashing down on the judge's stomach, knocking all the air out of his system. Katamoto tried to move while in shock, but the weight of Chico held him down while Sandi was holding his head and keeping his mouth shut, allowing Vicki to inject the poison into the side of his neck. Katamoto was no match for Chico and in a few minutes, his body began to convulse with a foam-like substance coming from his mouth through the fingers of Sandi as well as his nose. Soon his body went limp and the Star Chamber was down another judge.

Confirming that Katamoto was dead, the assassins admired the swimming koi and the numerous bonsai styled trees surround the pool. "If you are going to die, what a peaceful place to do it," Vicki said as she placed the syringe into her pocket. They took a few more minutes to admit the backyard and then retraced their steps, leaving without a trace.

Chapter Nine

Their lovemaking went on for hours. First it was passionate, and then it turned to animalistic. Exhausted, Jeannie laid in Ricky's arms playing with the hair on his chest. "God, I missed you. Here I was at the damn Super Bowl with your cousin, watching my 49ers blow their lead and eventually lose the game, and all I did was think of you."

"It's nice to be wanted," Ricky replied. "So, how bad was my cousin?"

Jeannie laughed and said that since Ricky could not be there, Ismail was the logical replacement. "That guy can eat, I'm telling you. Three hotdogs, one helping of nachos, and three beers. Oh, I forgot. He also got a hot sundae."

"That's my boy. And you know, he never puts on weight," Ricky said while laughing.

"I asked him about that, and you know what the little perv said?" Jeannie asked not expecting a response. "He said that when you have an Alpha-sex drive like him, the calories just naturally come off." Pinheiro started laughing so hard Jeannie had to get off his chest. "He said that?" Ricky asked, still laughing.

"You find that funny, do you?" Jeannie said will pinching one of Ricky's nipples.

"Ouch," Ricky yelled. "You know though, how many kids does my cuz have now?"

"Oh God, you are just as pathetic as him. Both Portuguese perverters," Jeannie said as she slid her hand down over Ricky's groin and found him hard again. After another round of lovemaking, there was an uneasy quiet now in the room, as if both Jeannie and Ricky were in deep thought.

Jeannie was the first to break the silence by asking Ricky what he was thinking about. "A hot chocolate sundae," he said laughing. "Do you want another pinch?" Jeannie asked starting for his right nipple again. "No, no, I was just kidding," Ricky said. He took a deep breath and said, "Gee, I didn't know you were into masochism." Jeannie successfully grabbed his groin and said that she could pinch there also. "No, no. Ok, I was thinking that I am falling in love with you. There, I said it." Jeannie did not know what to say.

"You're awful quiet," Ricky said as he placed his hand around Jeannie's waist and the other on the top of her head. Jeannie was laying on her back. Ricky then notices a tear falling from Jeannie's left eye. "Did I say something wrong?" he asked.

"No, it is not you. It's me," Jeannie said. "You know I am a two-time loser when it comes to long term relationships. I try to tell myself it's the job, the travel, the rush of trying to catch the bad guys, but maybe it is just me. Maybe I just don't understand what love is. Quiet again took over the room. "Come on big guy, what does love mean to you?" she asked. While taking a deep breath and now sitting up in bed with his back to the headboard, Ricky said that the best definition he ever heard about love, came from a man who called into a talk show hosted by a female psychologist whose name he forgot.

"There were some fruitcakes that called in saying that love was wanting to jump the bones of your significant other all the time. Other males said true love was having a wife that never got headaches when they were horny. And then a man called in and he had a hard time in what he was trying to say. His definition of love was being there when his wife discovered a lump on one of her breasts. Love was being with her when she visited her doctor who recommended a mammogram. Love was sitting next to his wife when the doctor recommended a biopsy. And love was waiting with his wife for the results which seemed to take days. Love was going to the doctor's office and learning with your wife that the biopsy came back malignant and that she needed to have an immediate mastectomy. Love is waiting at her side waiting for the anesthesia to wear off. And love is going with her to buy a specialty bra so no one knows she had one breast removed.

The caller got so choked up at this time that the psychologist told him to take a few breaths before continuing, which he did. He then continued by saying that love is being there when your wife's doctor informs her that the cancer has spread and that she needed to undergo chemotherapy. Love is sitting by your wife's side holding a bowl below her chin as she vomits from the chemo, and love is laughing with your wife as more and more of her hair falls out. The laughing continues as you and your wife select wigs which she hopes will not be needed when her hair grows back. Love is the joy you two share when the doctor tells you the cancer is in remission. The caller again choked up and got his composure back quickly this time. Love is when the doctor calls requesting to see your wife in his office. Love is learning that the cancer has returned. Love is watching your wife's weight tumble down as the treatments prescribed are not working. Love is being told that your wife needs to go into hospice. And finally, love is holding your wife's hand and hearing her last words of "I love you," before she goes with the angels.

"That is the best definition I have ever heard about what is love, and that is how I see it also,"

Ricky said. He turned to look at Jeannie to get a comment from her.

Jeannie was not sure when she lost it, but her mascara was running into her eyes, down her cheeks soaking the top sheet that she had used to cover her nakedness. She began to sob heavier and shake until Ricky pulled her into his arms and stroked her hair. She swung her right leg over his legs and said, "I love you so much," as they both fell asleep.

The next morning Jeannie woke to the aroma of something cooking in the kitchen downstairs. She grabbed her robe, pulled her hair back into a ponytail and decided to investigate. In the kitchen she found Ricky in his sweatpants and t-shirt, scrambling eggs while strategically keeping fried potatoes and linguica separate from each other. She entered the room at the same time the toaster popped up four slices of bread. Ricky had already called Amir at the hotel and told him to grab a cab and me him at the bureau since he had already gotten an early start.

"Good morning sunshine. I hope you are hungry," said Ricky with a big smile on his face.

"I am famished," Jeannie said. "You didn't have to get up and make breakfast, but I love it," she said.

"Wait until you taste it. You may hate it," he responded. He plated the breakfast on two plates, placed them on the kitchen table, and before sitting himself, poured two cups of coffee.

"God, this is so good," Jeannie said. "Linguica even. Your cousin would be proud of you."

"Well, you know, us alpha male-sex machines need to keep our weight off while restoring our vital nutrients."

"You are a pervert just like your cousin," Jeannie said as she placed another spoonful of breakfast into her mouth. Right on cue, Jeannie's cellphone went off on the counter where she had placed it the night before. Normally it is on her nightstand next to her bed, but passion got in the way last night, so her routine was off. She grabbed the phone and said to Ricky, "Speaking of the devil," while answering with a "Hey you, what's up."

"I know my cousin stayed with you last night, so I think I am supposed to ask what's up," he said, while trying to suppress a laugh. "God, both of you need to go into therapy," Jeannie said as she smiled at Ricky. "What did you find out?" she asked Ismail.

"Well, little bin Laden lives in a crappy flat on the third floor in the Haight. His room faces the rear, but he can only come and go through the front door. The place is not up to code since there is no fire escapes from either the second or third floor. His mailbox is blank, but I talked to a friendly who told me that Hassan recently moved it. Setting up surveillance shouldn't be too hard. There are a lot of homeless encampments on the street. You want to order surveillance now?

"Hang on one-minute while I check with Ricky," she said.

"Ricky is it? Must be getting serious," he said while laughing. "Shut up," Jeannie said as she got ready to relay the information to Pinheiro. She then returned to the phone and told Ismail to stay in the Haight until the surveillance team showed up. When they do, she told him to get back to the office.

"Roger that boss. Oh, and ask my cuz if he slept well last night?" Jeannie just hung up.

After breakfast they took a shower together and that led to another tumble in the hay before showering solo and getting ready for the drive across the Dumbarton Bridge into the city. Jeannie showered first and started to blow her hair dry but finally decided to just put it in a ponytail and be done with it.

Pinheiro walked outside while Jeannie made sure everything was locked up. With Ismail still having Jeannie's Vette, she left the bureau car in her driveway. She closed the front door and turned just in time to see Delores, her next-door neighbor and watchdog quickly converge on Ricky. "Hi, Jeannie. How are you?" Delores asked as she looked Ricky up and down. "And who do we have here?" she asked. Shit, Jeannie thought. The neighborhood gossip will make sure everyone knows she had a sleepover. She would have made a great minuteman during the American Revolution where she could have alerted the Continental Army that the British were coming.

"Hi Delores, I am fine. How are you?" Jeannie said, trying to avoid her initial question regarding Ricky.

"Hi, I am Ricky Pinheiro. I work with Jeannie from time to time," he said as he offered his hand to Delores. Delores began blushing and realized that she still had her oversized curlers in her hair.

"Oh, nice to meet you," Delores said. "I'm Jeannie's next-door neighbor," she said as she pointed out her house. "I watch Jeannie's house and put out the garbage when she is tied up. Well, I don't mean tied up," she said as she absentmindedly touching her curlers. "Oh my, I think it is going to be hot today," Delores said, fanning her face. "Well, you guys have a nice day, and don't forget Jeannie to let me know if you need anything. I will talk to you later." She turned and walked back to her house, stopping on two occasions to get a better look at Ricky.

"She seems nice," Ricky said as he got into the passenger front seat. "Ugh, you have no idea," said Jeannie as she got behind the wheel and began backing out of the driveway, seeing Delores looking out her front bay window pushing the Venetian blinds open just enough to get a better view.

With all six in the kitchen, Joey asked Chico, Vicki and Sandi, how the operation went with Judge Kanamoto. "It was a breeze," said Chico. "The old fart never knew what hit him." Sandi and Vicki nodded in agreement. "Good, two down and six to go," said Joey. He briefly left the room and returned with a 3' by 4' white cardboard piece of paper. He placed in on the table which had been cleared by Amy and Billy. "Here is the exterior and interior of Pavlenkos' house. Almost on the hour, you say you saw security personal walk outside, check the perimeter and sides of the house and then return inside, correct?" Vicki, Sandi, Billy, and Chico all agreed.

"That means there are only two inside the house with Pavlenko. This pattern does not seem to vary, only having new personnel arrive in twelve-hour shifts. This is good. Inside the house, on the second floor is the alarm system, monitored by one of the two inside guards. Pavlenko is normally in his third-floor study. Here is how we are going to do it."

Chapter Ten

Pinheiro held Jeannie's right hand during the drive from Newark to San Francisco. Traffic was heavy, so they were about thirty-five minutes late, but neither of them complained.

Pinheiro and Jeannie found Amir in the breakroom and just as they were getting seated, Jeannie's phone when off. It was Ismail. "What's up Ace?" Jeannie asked. "Hey, you are not going to believe this, but legal is asking you and me to meet with the scumbag judge, you know, Baldwin in federal lockup. He wants to make a deal and will give us some information about the Star Chamber and the Sons and Daughters of Liberty, the SDL for an easier sentence on the child porn rap. They want to know if we can attend a meeting with them and Baldwin at 1300 hours today. I told them that it should not be a problem but if so, I would call them back. "No, that should be ok," Jeannie said.

After disconnecting from Ismail, she told Pinheiro and Amir about the request. Pinheiro was familiar with the Star Chamber investigation and how the court disappeared along with this group of assassins identified as the enforcement branch of the court. To their knowledge, the SDL also went into hiding. Both he and Jeannie filled Amir in about the former investigation since his knowledge only came from the media. "I wonder what the prick will give up," Jeannie asked.

After a cup of coffee, Jeannie checked in with her receptionist, Tami, and gathered her phone messages. With Pinheiro and Amir in tow, they walked down to see if Lomax was in his office. He was not. Tami told them that Lomax was in the briefing room with Burk and Darcy. The three proceeded to the briefing room and saw Darcy and Burk pointing out items taped to the white-board. "Sorry for being a little late," Jeannie said. "Traffic was a bear this morning."

The three of them walked up to the white-board and saw that Burk and Darcy had been busy. The two of them had pretty much duplicated the display wall that was hanging in the Dallas field office. They had Google overhead photos of the front and rear areas of the apartment complex in the Haight. Ismail arrived and grabbed a cup of coffee and took a seat. Lomax confirmed that Jeannie had ordered a 24/7 tactical surveillance team in place. He then turned to Pinheiro and asked his opinion on how to proceed?

Jeannie got a closer look at the photograph of Hassan. There was something about the density of his eyes, they were like black holes where everything gets sucked in and nothing comes out, that suggested a hiding place for evil.

"First, I have to compliment your team for a great workup," Pinheiro said as he waved at the white-board. "We need to quickly set up a computer for Amir to re-establish his communication with Hassan. This will buy us some time and also allow your surveillance teams to record his movements here in the city."

Lomax looked at Jeannie who got the cue. "Ok, Darcy, Burke, why don't you take Amir and get him set up – whatever he needs. Ismail, take Ricky, I mean Pinheiro, in the Vette and let him see the lay of the land. I will alert the surveillance team that you two will be cruising the area. She then turned and became fascinated again with Hassan's photo. "Let's just hope that he has not already found a target and is ready to carry out his jihad."

It was the first time for Pinheiro to ride in Jeannie's hot Corvette. "So, you and boss lady got something going huh?" Ismail asked. Before he could answer, Ismail continued. "You know, she is not only a fantastic boss but probably my best friend besides my wife."

"First, if you are concerned that I will hurt her, you don't have to worry. I told her last night that I had fallen in love with her," Pinheiro said to his cousin.

"Wow, that's great," Ismail said. "I think you two would be good for each other. When's the big day?" he asked.

"Slow down cuz," Pinheiro said smiling and looking out the window. "We have only been together a short time, but there is a lot of chemistry between us. We haven't even discussed how to handle a long-distance relationship – you know how much I have to travel for the job and being stationed in D.C. We've decided to take it slow, but God, any chance I get to fly out here and see here, I volunteer. You know, they were going to send another agent instead of me, but I pulled rank just to be here with her."

"Sounds like you got it bad, brother," Ismail said as he ran through the gears of Jeannie's Vette. "We are getting close to Hassan's dumpy apartment. Hey, if we ever get some free time, I want you to bring Jeannie to our house for dinner. My wife would love that." "Sounds good to me. Maybe your wife will make me some malasadas. What do you think?"

Hassan's apartment was located on Oak Street. Ismail drove up and down the street three times so that Pinheiro could see the layout for all angles. "How the fuck could this prick afford an apartment here?" asked Ricky. "I mean, what is the rent here anyway?"

"Bro, some of these places go for over $8,000 per month. Can you believe it? And this is not even close to the nicest places in the city. I suspect, but until we get enough to get into his apartment, that he really is living in a large closet of an apartment without the landlord or owner being aware."

"What do you mean?" Pinheiro asked.

"See, it's like this. I rent an apartment for say $3500 a month. That's a lot of money for one person so, what I do is cleanout my closet and rent that space out for say $1500 a month helping me with the rent. The guy who rents it probably doesn't like it, but it beats commuting back and forth over the bridge to the east bay. In exchange for his rent, he has a place to sleep, bathroom and kitchen privileges, all without the landlord being aware. Knowing what I know about this fuck, he probably piggy-backs on the Internet service of the legal apartment renter and he is in business."

"Son-of-a-bitch. $1500 a month just to live in a closet. Unbelievable," said Pinheiro as he looked one last time at the complex. "How do you and Jeannie do it?" he asked. "Hell, like all the other agents in the San Francisco bureau, we had to find residences across the bay. We can't afford to live here. But actually, I wouldn't want to live is this shitty city anyway. The fucking liberal city government have turned the city into a third world country." Just then they saw a male pull down his pants near the curb and shit all over the sidewalk and street. "See what I mean?" Ismail said. "Do you know the SFPD don't even respond to car burglaries anymore? One of my friends on the force told me that they get a call regarding a car burglary every twenty-two minutes."

"Damn," said Pinheiro. "That's worse than D.C. but you know, that brings up something I did not think about, shit. How is Hassan getting around? Does he have a car, motorcycle or is he using public transportation?"

"I am sure our surveillance teams will let us know. Let's get back to the bureau, but since I have your girlfriend's car, I think we need to take the long way back," said Ismail and he gunned the Vette's engine.

"Agent Loomis, Flores, I am glad you could make it on such short notice," said Peter Stevenson, one of the best legal minds in the federal prosecutor's office in the city. "Let's go in here so we can talk before meeting with Baldwin and his attorney. Jeannie was glad Stevenson did not refer to Baldwin as a judge. He was a child rapist and pedophile and no longer deserved to be referred to as a magistrate in her mind.

"I got a call last night from his attorney, Andrew Kaufman, who said that his client wished to make a plea deal. As I told Agent Flores, he is willing to give up information about the Star Chamber and the, let's see (glancing at his notes), the Sons and Daughters of Liberty. I assume that would be of great interest to the FBI."

"Yes, it would," said Jeannie. "Our investigation came up short. When we hit the prior location of this secret court, they had already cleared out leaving no leads. The only information we had, came from our informant before he died. He was a member of the SDL."

"I see. Well, I don't want to be locked into a plea deal unless you two feel it is justified based on what he might provide. How about if we do this? I will inform him and his counsel that he has to give up something tangible before we can even discuss a deal. We will take a break and reconvene, and you can tell me what you think. Is that ok with you?" Stevenson asked. Jeannie and Ismail agreed.

Stevenson entered the slightly larger room followed by Jeannie and Ismail, after being allowed in by a uniformed officer. There sat Baldwin with a smirk on his face. Next to him was Kaufman, a sharply dressed young male probably in his mid-forties Jeannie thought. He rose and shook hands with Stevenson who introduced Jeannie and Ismail. Everyone took a seat and Jeannie could feel Baldwin's eyes staring at her instead of his counsel or the federal prosecutor. Still trying to intimidate huh asshole, she thought.

"Mr. Baldwin," Stevenson said. "It's Judge Baldwin, if you don't mind," said an obvious adversarial response from the former judge. Stevenson did not correct himself but instead continued. "Your attorney, Mr. Kaufman, has informed me that you wish to give up some information about the secret court known as the Star Chamber and the Sons and Daughters of

Liberty in exchange for a reduced sentence. Is that correct?"

Baldwin looked at his attorney before speaking. "That is correct," was his response. "Here is what I am offering. I will explain how the Star Chamber was formed, how it worked, and how the SDL carried out our verdict."

Stevenson looked at Jeannie and Ismail inviting them to speak if they wish. "I think you have to be a little more specific," Jeannie said. "We already have a lot of information about the Star Chamber and the SDL." Jeannie hoped that her bluffing would get Baldwin upset at which point he may blurt out something they did not know for free.

Instead, Baldwin laughed and leaned further back into his chair. "I doubt that Agent Loomis. I assume you and your colleagues raided the estate where the court held its sessions and found nothing. And, from what I heard, your only connection with the SDL was a now dead member. How am I doing?" he asked with a smirk on his face.

Jeannie did not response until she decided to use a different tactic. "Look, your honor, for several months, there has been no activity of the Star Chamber. Perhaps your members have decided to terminate the court, in which case, the investigation will, over time, become cold. If you want to play cat and mouse with us, I see no need to play, since nothing is happening. Should the Star Chamber start up again, the investigation will resume. Do you have time on your hands to wait until that happens?"

Jeannie's reference to Baldwin's former title seemed to boast his ego however temporally, but you could see that he was processing what Jeannie had said, especially her reference to how much time Baldwin had left in his life being in his early seventies.

Baldwin looked at Stevenson, then Jeannie and Ismail, and finally leaned forward and whispered something into his attorney's ear. "My client would like to talk to me in private before we proceed if that is ok?" he asked looking at the federal prosecutor. "How much time do you need," Stevenson asked. "No more than 10-minutes," came the response. Stevenson, Jeannie and Ismail returned to the smaller office where they first met. "You seemed to strike a cord Loomis. I think he might rollover now. How did you know that hitting him about his age would work?" Stevenson asked.

"I just figured that he is looking at what, minimum 15-20 years? That's almost a death sentence for him. That means a lot of years behind bars where he cannot molest young boys and girls."

"Do you think he is really going to give up anything useful or is he just pulling our chain?" Ismail asked, looking at Jeannie. "I wish I knew, but he is the one who asked for the audience with us," Jeannie replied. There was a knock on the door and upon opening it, there stood Kaufman. "Good job Agent Loomis. Your little use of psychology worked. My client is willing to cooperate with you."

Jeannie, Ismail and Stevenson followed Kaufman back into the room with Baldwin. Baldwin stared at Jeannie and Ismail, and then said, "Agent Loomis, you said something to the effect that the Star Chamber is out of service as well as the SDL. You are correct regarding the Star Chamber, but you mean the great FBI has not connected the dots about the most recent deaths of two other judges? Specifically Judges Swartz and Kanamoto? The SDL is still very active. What are my taxes paying for?" he asked smiling.

Jeannie looked at Ismail and then back at Baldwin. "Do you want to expand on your statement, or shall we continue to play ask a question and if I feel like it, I will respond?" Jeannie asked, returning a smirk smile. "Very well. I guess when you leave you will get all the gory details. Let me start from the beginning shall we. The Star Chamber has been in session for over two years. One of the most recent actions you are aware of Agent Loomis. In fact, your investigation caused the Seattle Police Department to reclassify an accidental death to a homicide.

"The former Secretary of State, Virginia McKenzie correct?" Jeannie said. "Exactly," Baldwin replied. "That was the work of the SDL?" she asked. Baldwin just nodded. "Also, do you two recall a drone attack on a mountain top chateau in the Swiss Alps? The one in which Horace Beaumont and his entire family were killed by VX gas?" Baldwin asked again. "I heard about it," said Ismail. "You are saying it was the SDL again?" "Yes," said Baldwin.

"Agent Loomis, did you and your colleagues on the Seattle Police force actually think that the SDL member that brilliantly killed Daniel Blackstone and Summer Tillson, the radical attorney at the roadside café was the only member of the SDL? Too bad he died before he could give you more information."

Jeannie's mind was in overdrive, and then it clicked. "So, what you are saying is that some SDL members are now, for whatever reason, killing judges who sat on the Star Chamber?"

"Not for some unknown reason," Baldwin laughed, "It is simply revenge. Let me spell it out for you so that you and your partner there can understand. When I was active in the Star Chamber, the SDL had nine members that I was aware of. They were both in the United States and abroad. Our sergeant-at-arms was their leader. He selected them and after a verdict was rendered, chose who would carry out our sentence."

"So, you acted as both the judge and executioner?" asked Ismael. Baldwin pressed one index finger to the other forming a teepee. He leaned forward and looked directly at Ismail. "Yes, we all did Agent Flores."

"And the name of the sergeant-at-arms is?" Jeannie asked.

"Joey. Don't ask me his last name. I don't think any of us knew it, but I could be wrong. What I do know is that he served two tours of duty in the Middle East, Iraq and Afghanistan if memory serves. He was in a black ops unit, very classified. The original judge who came up with the concept of the Star Chamber recruited him since he shared the same values as we do. If you like, I can talk about that?" Baldwin asked. "What is the name of that judge?" Ismail asked.

"Sorry Agent Flores, that is not part of the agreement," Baldwin quickly asserted.

"Joey was given free reign by the first magistrate to recruit other members and carry out sentencing however he so chose. But, after my arrest, the Star Chamber panicked and ordered not only the court to go dark temporality, but to get rid of any loose ends, which met that members of the SDL had to be eliminated. Three were killed almost immediately. One was responsible for the killing of the former Secretary of State, and the other two participated in the roadside café poisoning and the drone attack. Who the Star Chamber used to commit those assassination, I do not know since I was out of commission. If they went after Joey, I guess they were not successful. Joey obviously learned of the killings of his recruits and vanished with five other members."

"You said that Joey shared the same ideas of the Star Chamber judges. Can you explain that?" Jeannie asked. "Sure, Agent Loomis. I would be glad too," Baldwin responded. "Joey was the only SDL member who regularly attended sessions of the court. During breaks, he and I would occasionally talk. He is a very bright and articulate young man. I think he would have made a good jurist. Sorry, I digress. He was of the opinion that the liberals in our society have been allowed to occupy government offices in our major cities, Los Angeles, San Francisco, Baltimore, New York and so on, where they install their socialist ideologies contaminating those cities. Joey expressed his concerns about those cities having two types of law enforcement. One was for the rich and middle class since they had money, and the other was for those perceived to not have any. He said that the last time he was in Los Angeles, as an example, many of the streets downtown were filled with the homeless who crapped and urinated on the streets and sidewalks, yet no one is cited or arrested." Ismail remembered the male who defecated in front of him and Pinheiro just that day. "Mixed in with the homeless are street vendors cooking their food or selling merchandise on the sidewalks totally unregulated. No code enforcement is taking place by the city. Why? They do not have any money. But, a soccer mom driving her daughter to soccer practice in her Lexus gets pulled over for going 34 in a 25 mile per hour zone. Again why? Because she is perceived to have money.

The police don't like it, but they have to go along with the cities socialists' policies or lose their jobs. So, Joey and his recruits that made up the SDL, had no qualms about carrying out our sentences like Secretary McKenzie, Beaumont, etc."

"Who decided on where the Star Chamber meet?" Jeannie asked. "That was up to Joey. He had all of the judges' burner phones and notified them as to the location. We were all scheduled by Joey, to arrive at a different time, supposedly so we would not run into each other during our arrival or departure and learn each other's identity, but we eventually knew the names of our fellow judges even calling their last names during a call for their verdict. You know, Judge Swartz, "guilty," Judge Kanamoto, "guilty," and so on.

"Do you know how Judge Swartz and Kanamoto were killed" Jeannie asked. "No. The rumor mill inside this facility is not reliable. Sometimes we don't get any new news." Quickly, in hopes of tripping up Baldwin, Jeannie asked, "And the names of the other remaining judges are?" she asked acting as if she was about to write their names down on a piece of paper. "Nice try, Agent Loomis. Again, it is not part of the plea bargain. But, I would like to add something about Joey. Do not underestimate him. His IQ is off the charts. The military offered him a position in Army Intelligence if he re-enlisted, but he turned them down. I also heard that the CIA tried to recruit him before he went into the military, but again, that is only a rumor. When you think you have him, he will surprise you by being one step ahead."

Additional questions did nothing to further the investigation and so the meeting was preparing to break up, but Baldwin did not want to pass up the opportunity to pour vinegar into Jeannie's wound which he believed was still fresh. "Agent Loomis, I am so sorry that you were shot and lost your baby. I had nothing to do with that," he said with no hint of empathy. Jeannie felt the hurt but did not let on. "I would like to give you some information that I believe you and Agent Flores have wondered about for a long time. Who provided the layout of your Roseville substation? As a parting gift I will give you that individual's name." Baldwin waited for the right moment and finally said, "Your former SAC, Davenport, provided a lot of information to the Star Chamber when he was alive."

Jeannie and Ismail shook hands with Stevenson. "I hope the information he gave you helps your investigation," he said. "I think we got enough to re-open the case on the Star Chamber. How much time do you think he will get after the plea bargain?" Jeannie asked.

"He is still going to have to serve at least ten-years in federal prison but once others incarcerated there find out he is a pedophile, who knows what will happen to him."

Ismail and Jeannie got into the elevator. "Did Baldwin get too good of a deal?" Ismael asked. "No, I think we got a lot of good information, but I am not sure if we have anything concrete to follow-up on. I will fill in Lomax when we get back and give this information to Burk and Darcy, but we need to keep our focus on Hassan."

Chapter Eleven

"Unit one, the suspect is on the move walking west on Oak Street. We have two agents following him." "Roger that, unit one. Foot-surveillance team remember he already burnt the stakeout team in Dallas. Keep a loose tail and if you lose him, don't worry about it since we know where he lives," advised Pinheiro who was a passenger in a bureau car driven by Jeannie.

Hassan's walk was uneventful. He visited a street vendor and purchased something to eat and drink, and then walked back to his apartment. "Unit one, the subject has returned to his residence." "Shit, this could go on forever. We need to flush him out and see if he is the real deal as Dallas felt," said Pinheiro. "How are we going to do that?" Jeannie asked. "Let's go back to your office. I want to check in with Amir and see what the most recent emails from Hassan say. You might as well call my cousin in also. I think Hassan will stay in his apartment and hopefully get online."

Joey had everyone meet in the front room where he had the same piece of cardboard he used the previous night standing on a cheap easel showing the layout of Pavlenko's residence. "We will hit the house tomorrow night. I will schedule a meeting with Pavlenko for the afternoon. I will then call him and say I am running late, but that I really need to get his input about our plans for disrupting the upcoming Presidential fundraiser. He hates the President so much, that I know he will be eager to learn our plans. The butler will have already left for the day

After I gain entrance to the house, Amy and Billy will stroll hand-in-hand pass the front of the residence waiting for the two security guards to exit the house and perform their normal check of the perimeter. You, Sandi and Vicki, will be here next to the house next door hiding in the shadows," Joey said, pointing at Chico. No one reacts until you see my flashlight from the third-floor, understood?" Everyone acknowledged the order.

Once I am in the room with Pavlenko, I will make a request to see the Romanoff jewels. If he has them out on his desk like the last time, we got it made, but if not, I will get him to open the safe. Once the safe if open I will eliminate him. My next move will be to take out the security officer in the monitoring room. That leaves one security personnel left. I will track him down as if I was about to leave the house, like I have done several times. Once he is dead, I will go back upstairs to the third-floor and send you the signal. It is at that point that you three, Chico, Sandi and Vicki, will come out of the shadows and eliminate the two remaining guards outside. I will then open the front door. You three, plus Billy and Amy, will drag the bodies of the two dead guards into the house.

Vicki, you and Sandi try to destroy anything in the surveillance room that might connect us. Billy, Chico, Amy, you will meet me upstairs where I will be collecting the jewelry and money from the safe. Take anything else of value. Vicki, you and Sandi, when you are through in the room, start on the bottom floor and collect anything you feel we can use. Money, drugs, anything. We will all meet on the second floor giving it a once over. We should only be in the house for 20-minutes max and then off we go. Any questions? Alright we will leave here at 9:30. We will take the van and park it here. First out will be Billy and Amy, followed by me after I make the phone call. You three need to wait until you see me enter the house before taking your positions. If by chance the two guards come out side earlier than normal to check the perimeter, you two (pointing to Amy and Billy) have to really get it on so the guards will want to watch. Got it?" Joey asked. "Got it," Billy said, while Amy nodded. "Alright, let's check our weapons, suppressors and gloves. "Let's go people," Joey said as if he could hardly wait for the adventure.

As soon as Amir saw Pinheiro and Jeannie, he motioned them to come in and look at his monitoring screen where he typed in his translation with Hassan. Both were online and conversing with each other. Hassan told Amir in a boastful manner, that American intelligence had fucked up their surveillance in Dallas allowing him to escape capture. Amir congratulated him which inflated Hassan's ego. "Do you have a clean phone?" Amir asked. "Yes, I have two burner phones," came Hassan's answer. "Good, give me one of the numbers so I can call you tomorrow and set up a meet so we can formulate your plans, that is, if you still want to carry through with your jihad," said Amir. An irritated Hassan stated that he was more motivated than before and wished to get on with it or he would have to find someone else that could help him." He then complied and gave Amir the phone number to one of the burner phones. Hassan then stopped his conversation.

"Can you trace burner phones?" asked Ismail who entered the room and was watching the transcription on Amir's screen. "Yes," said Burk. "The carrier can," added Darcy. "They can trace any device that's actively on their network, whether they have GPS or not. The method is called Network-based tracking. The more accurate type is "Advanced Forward Link -Trilateration" followed by "Cell Tower Triangulation". Darcy blushed when she realized that a simple yes, would have sufficed.

Ismail looked at Pinheiro and said, "OK, now I know where you are going with this. If Hassan carries either of the burner phones when he is out and about, you can have the foot-surveillance team have a looser tail since the GPS will inform us as to his location if he gave them the slip. Nice." Pinheiro got a big grin on his face and said, "How can anyone doubt that we are related. Two great minds." "Oh God, give us a break," said Jeannie while Darcy and Burk looked at each other and broke into laughter.

Lomax entered the room as the laughter started to subside. "I have ordered Subway sandwiches and they should be here soon. Why don't we go into the briefing room?" he suggested.

As the group started their trek to the briefing room, Amir grabbed Pinheiro's arm, motioning him to stay back. "He is ready to explode," said Amir. "Sorry for the pun." "I know," said Pinheiro. "I have a plan, but I need to run it pass the FBI legal team. Jeannie," he called out, causing Jeannie to stop in her tracks and turn. "Is there a way you can request that someone from your legal department can meet us here in the break room as soon as possible?" Pinheiro asked. "Sure, I'll call them now. By the way, make sure you keep the SAC in the loop. He has a lot of powerful friends in D.C." "Good to know," said Pinheiro and he blew Jeannie an invisible kiss which she grabbed with her hand.

Colleen Day from legal showed up while everyone was finishing their sandwiches. "Gee, guess I am late," she said. "Not at all," said Lomax who offered her the remaining different types of sandwiches, chips and soft drinks. She helped herself while Pinheiro introduced himself, stating that he was with the Department of Homeland Security. "Wow, must be big," she said. Pinheiro gave her a synopsis of past and present events. "We understand that currently, with what we have, we would not be able to successfully obtain an arrest warrant. "Yes, you are correct," Day said matter-of-factly.

"Ok, here is what I am suggesting, Ms. Day."

"Please, call me Colleen," she said.

"Ok, Colleen, here is what we hope to accomplish. Grabbing a dry erase marker, Pinheiro walked up to the white-board and wrote the number one and a hyphen. "It is time for Hassan to reveal his true intentions beyond the rhetoric he has shared with Amir on-line and at the hotel. We will set up another meet similar to what your Dallas field office did. We have two rooms set up at a hotel downtown. Amir will continue to act as Hassan's al Qaeda mentor. Agents will be listening and recording in the next room. Amir will tell him that he will be provided with the tools he needs for his jihad. He will show him some photos of previously used large truck bombs and assorted handguns. This should force Hasson to make a selection of the tools that he wants. Amir will then ask him if he has chosen a specific target in the city. Everyone looked at each other while Day had her mouth open.

"You really aren't going to give this terrorist a bomb, are you?" Day asked.

"No, this is strictly to meet the requirements we need to secure the appropriate search warrants and know, once and for all, how dedicated Hassan is to committing his jihad.

"If Hassan performs as you hope he does, you have easily met the burden of proof and I think any jury will see that the motivation to kill came from him, not a federal law enforcement agency. I would easily sign off on this," Day said while taking a sip of coffee.

Joey showed up at Pavlenko's residence in the same fashion as before. One of the security officers, opened the front door, gave him a quick once over and allowed him to enter. If he had decided to frisk Joey, and discovered his weapon, Joey was prepared to react. Instead the security guard closed the door and walked over to the side of the entry and continued to watch a program on the television with his partner. Joey made note of their location and proceeded upstairs. On the second-floor two other security officers were looking and the monitoring equipment and never raised their heads as Joey walked by. By now, Billy and Amy should be strolling hand-in-hand on the sidewalk in front of the residence and Chico, Sandi and Vicki should be in the shadows.

Joey entered the room and saw Pavlenko working out on his NordicTrak treadmill. Be nice if you just died while working out you fat fuck, Joey thought, but then I could not get you to open the safe. He established eye contact with Pavlenko. "Joey, great job over in Berkeley. Your people did a good job shaking things up. I hear they had to cancel the show. Wonderful, wonderful. I hope you have something special for the President next month," he said as he slowed down the treadmill and prepared to dismount. Once the machine stopped, he grabbed a towel and began wiping the sweat off of his face. "Would you like some water?" he asked as he helped himself to a bottle of Acqua di Cristallo which Joey knew cost $60,000 per 750 ml. "No thank you," Joey replied. I wanted to discuss the plans for the President's fundraiser and give you a quote about how much I think it will cost." "Yes, yes, not a problem. I want it big and bad so all of the media outlets will have to broadcast it. Hurt some people, set some fires, make it big," Pavlenko said as he walked to his desk chair.

Joey outlined his plan and Pavlenko liked it. "I think I will need about $50,000 to set it up," he said. Pavlenko had started to open his side desk drawn where Joey knew he kept some cash, but Joey had hoped, that requesting such a large sum, Pavlenko would have to open the safe, which is exactly what he did.

Pulling his silenced semi-automatic from the back of his waistband, Joey fired one round into Pavlenko's knee while placing his hand over his mouth to quiet his scream. He told Pavlenko that he would be killed if he did not write down the combination to the gun vault. Pavlenko looked up at Joey and knew that if he did not comply, he would be killed. Gimacing in pain, he reached to his desk and after grabbing his pen, wrote out the combination. Having his back to Joey, he never saw Joey pull the trigger, firing a round into the back of his head. He banged his head into the safe's door before falling on the floor. Joey took a quick look into the safe, saw the jewelry and two large stacks of bills. He turned and began walking down to the second floor. There he found the two interior guards looking at the monitoring equipment while engaged in some conversation. As they turned to look at Joey, it was too late. Two quick bursts from his weapon hit both guards in their chest. He finished them off with two head shots. Returning to the third-floor study, he turned on his small flashlight he had in his front pocket and pointed it out the window.

Vicki and Sandi saw the light and started towards the guard walking from their side of the house. Chico saw them advanced and did the same from his side. With little effort they took out the last two guards taken by surprise. Chico was able to single-handedly pull his downed guard to the front door. Once there, he went over and helped Vicki and Sandi pull their much heavier victim near the front of the house and left him on the sidewalk until they could get Chico's guard into the house. Joey opened the front door and helped Chico with the first body. They returned and pulled in the second.

"Ok, let's start searching the areas you were assigned," said Joey, who returned to the third-floor. In the safe he found in excess of $150,000 plus a handgun and the Romanoff jewelry he had seen a few days earlier. Grabbing a pillow case from Pavlenko's bed, he first placed the cash followed by the jewelry. Chico found a gun vault containing so many weapons the group had to make two trips to get them all to the van. Pavlenko had AK-47s, AR 15s, assorted semi-automatics and a ton of ammunition. Vicki and Sandi destroyed the recording equipment and felt safe that nothing useable was left for law enforcement. The decision was made that the cash, jewelry and weapons were enough of a haul so other valuable items were left behind. In twenty-five-minutes the entire group was out of the house.

Chapter Twelve

Two days later an excited Hassan arrived at the Hilton Hotel in the financial district, again using a Lyft driver. Amir answered his knock and invited him to enter the room. He had previously listed online several of his possible targets and they were all located in this part of the city. He was focused on the financial infrastructure of the United States expressing that a successful attack on any of the financial institutions he had targeted would cause the U.S. economy to implode. He wanted a bomb big enough to bring down a building similar to 9-11, but he had neither the knowledge to build a bomb nor finance to purchase one. Pinheiro, Jeannie, and Ismael were in the adjacent room with the transcriber. Amir had to walk the tight-rope when he said that al Qaeda would provide the truck bomb, making sure that the suggestion first came from Hassan. Amir never suggested violence first, always giving Hassan a way out.

At first, Hassan said that he wanted to hit multiple targets similar to what he had seen by al Qaeda in the Middle East. He talked about placing backpacks at the airport, shopping malls, and sporting events, setting them off with a cellphone. Then he paused and took out a folded piece of paper from his rear pocket and said, "First, I want to bring this building down." It was a skyscraper housing one of the nation's largest credit card and banking institutions. "I will park a truck inside here, (pointing to the underground garage) and once I am clear, I will remotely detonate the bomb. I need a big bomb to bring the building down. I do not want something to happen like the first bombing of the World Trade Center.

"My brother," said Amir, "My superiors feel that you should concentrate on one large target first so that you will tie up the resources of the American police. Then while they are investigating the bombing of this building, you can hit your other targets." Hassan agreed, saying again and again that he wanted to impress the new leader of al Qaeda.

"Here are some pictures of truck bombs we have used in both Iraq and Afghanistan," said Amir, who passed the photos over to Hassan. Quickly, Hassan pointed to both pictures and said this is what he needed. "When can you get me the truck bomb?" he asked.

Pinheiro anticipated this request and told Amir to tell Hassan that a bomb this big would take one-week to build. Hassan did not seem disappointed but asked how he should do it?" Amir suggested that once the bomb was made and secured in the back of a truck, the two of them could meet. He asked Hassan if he had a car? Hassan quickly said he would get one. "Fine," said Amir. "It will take our brothers one week to build such a bomb. After you get a car, find directions to the San Francisco Zoo by Golden Gate Park. I will call you and tell you where I am parked with the truck once it is ready. You can take whatever route you want to your target and I will follow to pick you up once you have it parked." Hassan had a huge smile on his face shaking his head excitedly up and down. His dream of jihad was almost ready. He shook Amir's hand and quickly left the hotel.

Lomax, per request of Pinheiro, contacted both the FBI's own bomb squad, the SFPD tactical team as well as the U.S. Army requesting their best bomb technicians to meet at the bureau the next day. They then discussed how to create a non-destructive bomb big enough to impress Hassan who may have knowledge regarding the type of bomb needed to bring down a building. Working almost none stop, the bomb experts began assembling the device.

Amir told Pinheiro that he had an additional idea that should cement any conviction of Hassan once he was taken into custody. He would suggest to Hassan that he should make a video recording of his desire for jihad, which upon successful detonation of the device, would be sent to the new al Qaeda leader. Pinheiro felt that this was an excellent idea. Meeting two days later, Hassan sat in front of a video camera operated by Amir, wrapped in a cloth wrap around his face only showing his eyes. For seventeen-minutes, Hassan told his intended audience in the Middle East how proud he was to be a soldier of al Qaeda and already took credit for the attack that he would soon unleash on America.

Five days later, driving a cheap used Ford Focus, Hassan drove to the San Francisco Zoo. Parking on Sloat Blvd, he saw Amir standing by the side of a truck far away from other parked vehicles. Hassan parked behind the truck and approached Amir. Pinheiro and Ismael were parked across the street in a van having a two-way mirror on its side. The two of them were to the side of an agent recording the meeting who also interpreted what was being said. Amir looked up and down the street and then pulled up the tarp covering the bed of the truck. Hassan's eye became wide and he again sported a huge smile. The bomb covered the entire bed of the truck and even to Amir, looked extremely real. He then handed Hassan a cellphone telling him the number that needed to be dialed for detonation. He and Hassan exchanged keys at which point Hassan climbed into the cab of the truck while Amir did the same in Hassan's vehicle.

The surveillance teams were advised that the suspect was now in the truck and the tracking of the jihadist's started toward his intended target. Ismail, driving a bureau car drove parallel to Hassan on side streets. Jeannie did the same on the opposite side of the route Hassan was taking with Pinheiro in the passenger seat handling the radio.

Hassan arrived at his target and drove the car inside the parking garage. Amir followed behind. Hassan found a parking spot in the middle of the lot and parked. He got out of the truck, locking the doors with the key fob, and walked back to the passenger side of his vehicle and got in. Amir then drove Hassan to the rooftop parking of a building across from the credit card building which would allow Hassan to see his jihad take place. It would provide him with a perfect view of the destruction that would take place once he dialed the number. He did not notice that there were several occupied cars already parked on the roof of the building.

Hassan quickly jumped out of his car as did Amir. He looked across the street to his target and pulled the cellphone from his pocket. He smiled at Amir and dialed the number and pressed send. Nothing happened. He pressed send again getting the same result. He continued to press send not noticing that seven heavily armed individuals dressed in black and armed with assault rifles were running towards him. "Get down, get down," he heard as he turned and saw the FBI tactical team advance on them both. Hassan, still holding the cellphone and repeatedly pressing the send button was placed on the ground next to Amir. He did not stop pressing the send button until his hands were placed behind his back and he was cuffed. Pinheiro walked up and with a gloved hand, picked up the cellphone.

Jeannie walked up to Pinheiro and said, "Congratulations, Washington will be impressed." Before he could respond, Ismail yelled out, "Hey, what about me. I helped a little bit and if medals are going to be awarded, I want one." Jeannie and Ricky laughed and then he said, "That's my cousin."

Chapter Thirteen

Everyone at the San Francisco bureau celebrated with Pinheiro, Ismael, and Jeannie as they returned to the office. "Great job," Lomax said as he shook Pinheiro's hand. "Couldn't have done it without your team sir," came Pinheiro's response. "Debriefing can wait until tomorrow morning, say 10:00 a.m. I will have media relations write up something if they are contacted by the press. I think the way it went down, they have no clue. Ok, see everyone tomorrow."

The three of them walked to the elevator leading to garage. Ismail kept all of them laughing when he talked about Hassan repeatedly pushing the send button. "It reminded me of all of those Roadrunner cartoons. You know, Wile E. Coyote. He sees the Roadrunner coming and, at what he thinks is the precise moment, pushes down on the plunger to detonate the Acme Dynamite, and nothing happens. He does it over and over again, just like Hassan and the phone. I mean, I will never forget his pushing as hard as he could on the send button as our guys swoop down on him."

Reaching their cars, Ismael sees Ricky heading towards the passenger side of Jeannie sportscar. "Hey, you two, don't do anything that I will be doing when I get home," Ismael said, more for Jeannie's benefit than Pinheiro. "God, I hope when you get home, Bianca has a headache, Jeannie said. "Not going to happen," he said. "Once I take off my clothes and she sees this USDA prime body, she can't resist."

"Goodnight Ismael," Jeannie said while shaking her head. "Good night boss, goodnight cuz," Ismail replied as they both drove their cars out of the garage. "Hungry?" Ricky asked as he put his head on the headrest and closed his eyes. "Yes, and you?" Jeannie answered. "Yeah, you know Ismail told me of this great restaurant in the city called, Uma Casa on Church Street. Maybe we can go there?" "Why am I not surprised that Ismael recommended one of the best Portuguese restaurants in the city?" Jeannie replied. "Sure, that sounds like fun," she said as she made an illegal U-turn.

When they arrived, Jeannie was surprised to find a table in the corner available. "Gee, this is nice," she said as they sat. She did not notice the host wink at Ricky. He ordered a Sangria Vermehlo while Jeannie ordered a white port. On the other side of the dining room three guitar players made music for the diners.

Fortunately, it was not too noisy for Ricky and Jeannie to talk to each other. Jeannie raised her glass and toasted Ricky for a job well done. "You too," he said, as they clang their glasses together. After taking a sip of her wine, Jeannie excused herself to visit the ladies' room. When she returned, she picked up her glass and was about to take another sip when she saw it on the bottom of the glass – a diamond engagement ring. She looked at Ricky and back at the ring. She started to cry. "Oh God, here we go with the Hallmark moment thing," Ricky said, as he pulled out his handkerchief and handed it to her. "I am too tired to get down on my knees, but will you marry me?" he asked. Jeannie did not reply but instead placed her fingers into the wine glass and fished out the ring. She then handed it to him, causing him to feel that she was going to refuse. "What, are you saying no?" he asked. "No, you fool, you need to put it on my finger, and yes, I will marry you." On cue, the three guitarists came over to their table and played some song that neither Jeannie nor Ricky would ever be able to recall.

The next morning, they both woke in Jeannie's bed to a knocking on the front door. They both grabbed their cellphones to see if perhaps they had missed incoming calls. Neither of them had. Jeannie and Ricky dressed quickly. Jeannie put on a robe hanging of the inside of the master bathroom door. Ricky put on his sweatpants and t-shirt. Both grabbed their guns and headed downstairs were someone was persistently knocking on the door. Jeannie opened the door with Ricky standing by her side. Both of their handguns behind their back.

"Oh, you are home. I was so worried. I saw on Fox and Friends this morning that you two arrested a terrorist in San Francisco. My word, what is the world coming too?" asked Delores, still in curlers. "Oh, how rude of me. Hello Mr. Pinheiro. How are you?" Delores asked blushing and again, absentmindedly touching her curlers. "We are fine Delores. So, it's already on the news?" Jeannie asked. "Oh yes, on all the stations, but I only watch Fox News. I can't stand those other fake news channels. Well, I don't want to impose so I better get home. I just wanted to make sure you were safe. Bye!" And with that, the neighborhood queen of gossip and neighborhood watchdog walked back to her house.

Jeannie closed the door. Ricky broke into a deep, rich and infectious laughter. Jeannie laughed along with him causing them both to cry so hard that tears formed in their eyes. Jeannie wrapped her arms around Ricky and the laughter got even louder. "Oh my God," Jeannie said. "What"? replied Ricky. "I hope she didn't see my engagement ring. If she did, everyone in the neighborhood will know by lunchtime guaranteed. They looked at each other and broke out in laughter again.

Chapter Fourteen

"So, these items used to belong to the last Czar of Russia huh?" asked Vicki who, next to Joey, was the most intelligent of the group having attended college almost non-stop since graduating early from high school.

"That's what Pavlenko told me," said Joey. "He said that back in 1922 they were estimated to be worth north of $500 million." Everyone looked at the Romanoff jewelry, but most were concentrating on their share of the cash taken from Pavlenko's safe – which totaled to $150,000, or $25,000 apiece. Joey divided up the money and gave everyone their equal share. "Everyone happy?" he asked, not expecting any negative responses, and none came.

"Enjoy, but tomorrow we continue with our mission of revenge for our slain comrades and also my plan for the Sadler affair, SLA style."

Jeannie and Ismail caught up with the SAC and Pinheiro in the briefing room. Jeannie grabbed a leftover soda and half of a sandwich while Ismail took a bottled water. "How did it go?" asked Lomax. "Lots of information to fill-in the blanks about the Star Chamber investigation, but nothing concrete to act on immediately. He was our main threat," she said, pointing at the picture of Hassan on the white-board.

"I agree, but I need to pull Ismail off for a few hours to liaison with the SFPD. While you two were at the plea-bargain meeting, they responded to multiple homicides at Anatoly Pavlenko's mansion in Pacific Heights. Five dead including Pavlenko himself. It looks like a professional hit. Flores, I told them you would be there as soon as you returned from your meeting. "Yes sir," said Ismail and he headed out the briefing room.

"FBI Agent Flores," Ismail said to a stationed SFPD officer as he walked towards the crime scene tape. The officer logged Ismail name into his logbook and lifted up the tape. "Flores," shouted Paul Freeman, a long-time homicide detective who knew Ismail for years. Ismail walked up to him and shook hands. "Heard you got a big one," Ismail said. "Actually, it couldn't have happened to a better guy," Detective Freeman said. Ismail pulled a pair of latex gloves from his pocket while Freeman handed him covers for his feet. While putting the protective coverings on, Freeman said, "Five bodies in the house, but we found dragged marks and blood from the outside into the foyer of the place. Pavlenko's body is on the third floor. Two security guards got hit in the security monitoring room which, by the way, was trashed. You will see the first two right inside the front door laying on the marble floor."

Freeman opened the door and immediately Ismail saw two middle-aged white males who looked Russian laying face up with entry wounds in the center of their foreheads. "Each took one in the chest and a coup de grace shot to make sure they were dead. Let me tell you how I see it before we do the walkthrough and see if you agree," Freeman said. "These two got it outside. I think it had to happen after the events in the house since the monitoring crew would have seen it.

Someone had to have already gained entrance into the house and later opened the front door. "Hey, is that a Renoir?" asked Ismail pointing to a picture hanging on the wall accented by lights. "Flo, I didn't know you were an art aficionado," replied Freeman. "But, you are right. It's the real deal worth about twenty-five million. The thing is, it was stolen by the Nazis in World War II and had never been seen until it turned up here. If you like that one, wait until you see the art on display in the rest of the mansion."

Reaching the second floor Freeman took Ismail to the monitoring room where two more bodies were located. "This guy took two in the chest and was standing when he got hit. The guy seated has two headshots. One in the forehead and one behind his right ear. We haven't found any brass so they must have collected the spent shells.

On the third floor, Ismail saw another Renoir and paintings by Raphael and Hans Memling. "Stolen by the Nazis also?" Ismail asked. "Yep," came the response from Freeman. "Over there is a bust going back to the time of Cleopatra." Ismail saw the wall safe open and the dead body of Pavlenko laying on the floor. Whatever content was inside was long gone. "Wonder how much was inside here?" Ismail asked. "Wait till you see what we believe is missing in the next room," replied Freeman and he escorted Ismail.

The room had been a dedicated exercise room with numerous exercise equipment. Instantly Ismail focused on a large state of the art gun vault with the doors opened. The vault had been cleaned out of whatever might have resided inside. "This is the Sportsman double-wide series gun vault capable of holding 12 assault rifles, maybe AKs since he was Russian, nine pistols or semis, and 4-5 high powered sporting rifles. Dust on the floor shows the outline of what we think were ammo boxes."

"Just what we need. A bunch of killers with firepower better than us," Ismail said.

"Look at this view," Freeman said walking out onto the rooftop terrace off the exercise room. "Pavlenko had a million-dollar view. Probably more than that. He had this place on the market for a little while, dropping the price from $46 million down to $34," said Freeman. "Hell, when it is not foggy, he could have seen Alcatraz Island."

"Motive?" asked Ismail.

"Greed, revenge, shit who knows. A guy as wealthy as him, I'm sure had a lot of enemies."

"Can we go back to the monitoring room?" Ismail asked. "Be my guest," said Freeman and they went down one floor. It appeared to Ismail that someone removed the hard drives besides just trashing the place. "I was hoping that maybe they slipped up and left something behind that our forensic computer team could analyze, but they knew what they were doing."

"You know Ismail, they did forget to thoroughly check his desk. He had a hidden drawer that unless you really searched, you wouldn't find it. We did and found his laptop, but it's encrypted.

"Hey, if you fill out a chain of evidence sheet, I can take it back to our geek squad and let them try to break in. They were able to crack Judge Baldwin's computer in the Star Chamber case. "Great," said Freeman who called out to someone named Virgil. Bring over the laptop and a chain of evidence form, will you?"

"Thanks. I will let you know if they are able to get in and what, if anything, is found."

"Hope you do since right now I've got squat and the press will be all over us soon," Freeman replied.

Pinheiro walked into Jeannie's office carrying two cups of coffee. "Thought you might need this, "he said while yawning. "Yeah, I do. Someone kept me awake most of the night," she said while grabbing the cup. Just then, Darcy and Burk entered Jeannie's office. "Hey guys, I have something for you to work on now that we cleared the DHS terrorist's case."

"Oh, that hurts," said Pinheiro, laughing. "But, I have to admit, if it wasn't for the FBI's help, God knows what could have happened. "I can leave you three alone if you want," he said. "No, that's ok. Maybe you might have some thoughts about how we should proceed with the new information Baldwin gave Ismail and me. It's about the Star Chamber case.

Before Jeannie could brief Burk and Darcy, Ismail arrived carrying Pavlenko's laptop and evidence chain document. "Hey, you guys having a party and I didn't get invited?" he asked. "How bad was it at Pavlenko's house?" Jeannie asked. "Whoever whacked him and his security team knew what they were doing," Ismail said. Looking at Burk and Darcy, he said, "I have something for you two. It's Pavlenko's laptop but it is encrypted. The SFPD found it in a secret drawer of his desk. I volunteered you two experts and they gladly accepted our help. Here is the evidence log."

Darcy took the laptop from Ismail and then turned her attention back to Jeannie. "I know this is a shot in the dark, but Ismail and I got some new information from Baldwin." She, along with Ismail, filled in Burk and Darcy with the latest from the disgraced judge. "Not much to go on," said Burk. "Someone named

Joey, white male, in his thirties, former military, black ops in the Army.

"I know, but Ismail, can you come further into the room and close the door?" Jeannie asked. Ismail did as requested. "What I am going to tell you stays in this room. She quickly established eye contact with everyone including Pinheiro. "Baldwin told us that SAC Davenport was the individual who provided the layout of our Roseville office and the staffing that would be present when the place was hit by those three assholes.

"What? That fucker," Darcy said, quickly feeling color flood into her cheeks. "Oh, I am so sorry for swearing." "No need to apologize, that's what that prick was," said Ismail. "Can you two work backward, you know, check his computer usage, cellphone and bank records? Maybe we will get lucky," Jeannie said.

"With pleasure. Anything else?" Burk asked as he and Darcy prepared to leave Jeannie's office. "No, that's all I got. Jump on Pavlenko's computer first. If there is something that can help the SFPD, let's find it," Jeannie said as the two departed. "Hey," said Pinheiro. Anyone else hungry?" he asked looking at this watch. "I am," said Ismail, but if you two were planning on a "nooner" here in Jeannie's office, I would understand."

"You are right," Pinheiro said looking at Jeannie. "My cousin is a pervert." The three left heading to the IHOP around the corner for lunch. Ismail again congratulated both of them on their engagement. "I told you, boss, that once you have a Portaguee, you can't go back." Jeannie laughed but instead of a joking comeback said, "so true," while sporting a huge smile on her face.

"The wifey wanted me to ask if there is a date set yet?" Ismail asked.

"We just got engaged," Ricky said, while smiling at Jeannie.

"What I would like to do after we take the new information from Judge Baldwin as far as we can, is for the two of us to head up to my cabin in Coeur d' Alene and relax. Then we can make plans. What do you think?" Jeannie asked while leaning into Ricky, who agreed.

The next morning Ismail, Pinheiro, and Jeannie were in the briefing room removing the items from the Hassan investigation from the white-board while eating bagels and coffee. Lomax joined them briefly asking Jeannie for any updates. She brought the SAC up to speed, even though they really didn't have much new information.

Ismail's cellphone went off. He glanced at the display and said it was Darcy. "Yeah Darcy, what's up?" he said into the phone. "No shit! We're on our way." Looking at Ricky and Jeannie, Ismail told them that not only did Burk and Darcy get pass the encryption, but they found security files showing all of the murders. Pavlenko was spying on his security staff."

Chapter Fifteen

"This warehouse should fit the bill," Joey said to Amy while sitting in a second car used by the group. "Kinda shabby don't you think," said Amy. "Yeah, but it fits our purpose on two counts. First, after I re-establish contact with the remaining Star Chamber justices, explaining why I went into hiding, I will suggest that for the first new session of the court, we do not want to draw attention – thus this warehouse. Secondly, I don't think the cops care about such as shitty place, so we should be able to come and go with the furniture from the last Star Chamber location that we cleared out and stage the warehouse before it goes into session. OK, let's go, we need to stop at one more place," said Joey.

Jeannie, Pinheiro, and Ismael entered Darcy and Burk's computer lab. SAC Lomax was leaning over Burk and Darcy's shoulders fixated on their large computer screen. "I can't believe it. It really shows the killings?" asked Ismail. "Yes, it does, and his system also provides audio," Burk responded. Lomax back away allowing Ismael, Pinheiro, and Jeannie to view the screen. Pressing a button, Burk filled the screen with a male being allowed entrance into the mansion. The male is then seen going up the various floors until he reaches the third-floor where Pavlenko is seen exercising on a treadmill. "Joey, so nice to see you," he is overheard saying. "Joey," shouted Jeannie while looking at Ismail. "What are the odds?" she asked.

"I have already transferred funds to your off-shore account my friend for your next mission. This is only for you. I will give you whatever necessary funds you need for your recruitment exercise. I was very impressed in how you screwed up the U.C. event the other night. Very impressed. By the way, there is an upcoming event in the Senate over his impeachment. I want as many protestors as possible outside creating havoc with the police, calling for his downfall." "Understood. You will not be disappointed," Joey said.

"This is the guy who is either the leader or one of Antifa's main go-to guys," said Pinheiro. "Now we have evidence as to who sponsors their activities. Of course, it doesn't do us any good now that Pavlenko is dead."

"How is your side job going Joey?" Pavlenko was heard asking. "Side job?" said Joey. "Yes, I see Judge Kanamoto died recently. Your handy work again, dah?"

"Oh my God," Jeannie said excitedly while looking at Ismail. He is part of the SDL and Star Chamber." Everyone in the room watched Burk maneuver through the various files he had imported from Pavlenko's laptop on to his. The outside video did not pick up anything other than the muffled shots from four killers, two males and three females that were seen coming out of the shadows shooting the exterior guards who had no time to react.

Joey was seen entering the monitoring room and eliminating the two interior guards. Neither of them had a chance to clear their weapon. He is picked up again opening the front door and allowing the other five people from outside to enter. The rest of the video showed them systematically going floor to floor collecting values and several trips to move all of the weapons from the gun vault. No one spoke while the files were being viewed.

Silence was broken by Ismail saying that he needed to get ahold of Detective Freeman, saying this is going to make his day. He left the room as he was retrieving his cellphone. Pinheiro looked at Lomax and made a suggestion. "We still do not know their identities, but I have an idea. With your permission, I would like to connect Darcy and Burk with a friend in the DOD (Department of Defense). "Go for it," came the response from Lomax.

Removing his cell phone, he dialed a number from his directory and waited a few seconds. "Hello,

Miranda?" he asked. "Ricky Pinheiro. Fine, fine and you?" he asked. "Great. Hey, I am working a case with the FBI and the San Francisco Police Department. Yeah, the Pavlenko murders, how did you know? Already? Gee, when the media gets a hot story they are off and running before the bodies are cold. Listen, we found in a hidden desk drawer, Pavlenko's laptop. Two of the FBI's finest," he said while smiling at Darcy and Burk, "got passed his encryption and, get this, found security files showing all of the killings taking place with audio. No, I'm serious. About time we get some breaks huh? Here is what I am hoping you can do for us. Wow, two great minds think alike. Yes, I will have the two FBI computer forensic members connect with you and they will send you the files. Let me put Darcy on the line and you two can work out the details. I owe you Miranda, big time. Ok, here is Darcy." With that he handed his phone to Darcy, and as she began talking to Miranda, turned to Lomax, Burk, and Jeannie.

"Miranda and her team are experts in facial recognition. I am having Darcy send the files of all of the suspects to her so she can run them through their various systems. Name a data bank and she can access it. DoD, Interpol, FAA, Passport control – it's amazing what she can find.

"How long do you think it will take her?" asked Lomax. "She will probably get a hit quickly on this Joey character if it is true he was in the U.S. Army.

DMV data should come up with most of the others if they ever had a driver's license or identification card," Pinheiro said.

"Hello, Judge Silverman? This is Joey. Yes, Joey, your former sergeant-at-arms. How are you?" Judge Silverman was a little suspicious and very cagey in his conversation. "I want to apologize for going into hiding but you understand that when the decision was made by you and your fellow magistrates to terminate the court temporarily, I naturally panicked and went underground so to speak. Yes, I am aware of the recent deaths of Judge Swartz and Kanamoto. Sad, since they had done great work on the Star Chamber. Do you feel the other judges feel secure enough to start up the court again, because if you are, I have found a temporary location and can quickly set it up for the court." Judge Silverman said that several of the judges had been discussing starting up the Star Chamber again and he sounded intrigued with Joey's proposal. He asked Joey to give him a few days and he would poll the other members of the court and get back to him. Joey felt that Silverman took the bait and will convince the other judges to meet.

Forty-five minutes later, Joey arrived at a small home located in Alameda. He parked in the driveway since parking was at a premium. The person he wanted to see, rented as a residence, the detached garage located to the rear side of the main residence. "Shalam," Joey said to a college-aged Arab male coming out of the side garage door. He had seen Joey approach from the single window of the garage. "Shalam," came the reply as they both shook hands. The Arab invited Joey into the garage which was sparsely furnished with a small flat-screen television set, a used couch which was opened displaying a bed, and a small kitchen table that had a portable microwave. "Sit, sit. Would you like some tea?" he asked Joey. "Yes, that would be great," Joey said.

"What brings you to me?" he asked, while pouring bottled water into a teapot and securing two coffee cups.

I need three bombs capable of leveling a 25,000 square foot warehouse and incinerate anything inside. The bombs need to fit into three ceramic flower pots, 10.5 inches wide and 16" tall. I need a detonation device so that I only need to dial one number that will activate all three bombs."

He looked at Joey and while pouring the tea into Joey's cup said, "What you have requested I can provide in four days. The cost is $5,000. I hope that is not a problem?" Joey indicated that he would bring the money in four days.

Chapter Sixteen

At 3:15 p.m., Burk tracked down Jeannie who was with Pinheiro and Ismail in the breakroom. "Miranda got some ids already," Burk said. The three followed him to the large briefing room where Darcy was taping photos on the large white-board and then writing the name of the person under each photo. "Detective Freeman is on his way," said Ismail to no one specific.

One picture showed Joey, identified as Joseph Alan Rogers, 36-years old. He was in uniform displaying his rank as sergeant. Most of the other photos appeared to have come from the Department of Motor Vehicle licensing agencies. Another picture showed a Victoria Reynolds, 42 -years old. She looked like a 1960's college radical. The picture of an obese Mexican-America had the name Armando "Chico" Fernandez, age 27. Amy Nelson was a very pretty girl with large brown hair. She could easily pass as a high school student and was the baby of the group at only 18-years old. The photo of Sandi Marie Osborne showed a young woman who was or had been battling acne on her face. She displayed no smile in her photo. She was listed as being 25-years old. Finally a photo named William "Billy" Wagner rounded up the rows of the now identified killers of Pavlenko and his security team. Billy was 24-years old. His photo was from the California Department of Corrections – his booking photo.

"We should have a lot of background information to share by tomorrow morning," Darcy said. "Miranda and her team are awesome," she added. Just then Detective Freeman and his partner arrived. "Hey Freeman, let me introduce you to everyone," Flores said. Upon completing the introductions, Lomax entered followed by two of the new replacement agents carrying disposable coffee carriers, paper cups, sugar, and crème. "Thought we might need this," he said.

Everyone but Darcy helped themselves to the beverage.

"Ok," Lomax said. "Let's go around the room and see what we do know so far." Jeannie started by saying that Joey, Joseph Alan Rogers, was allowed entrance into Pavlenko's mansion while Victoria Reynolds, Sandi Osborne, Victoria Reynolds, and Billy Wagner waiting in the shadows on the side of the residence. The security files then showed Joey going upstairs where he finds Pavlenko exercising. Pavlenko goes to his safe and that is when Joey shot him in his knee. Joey is seen placing his hand over Pavlenko's mouth and later, Pavlenko is writing something on a piece of paper. When he finished, Joey shot him in the head. We assume he used a suppressor since the security team in the monitoring room did not respond to the third-floor."

"That makes sense," said Freeman. "Patrol units contacted all of the adjacent neighbors and no one heard any gunshots. That means the four killers outside used suppressor also."

Jeannie continued. "Joey goes to the second-floor and takes out the crew in the monitoring room. He is now home free. The file shows that he goes to a window facing the street and flashes a light signaling the four outside to take out the exterior guards. Amy joins the group. He then comes downstairs and opens the front door. They drag the two dead guards from the front inside the residence and then start cleaning out the property including Pavlenko's wall safe on the third-floor and the massive gun vault."

"That is how we wrote up our report for the DA. They will be issuing warrants by this afternoon for five counts of homicide on each of those individuals," Freeman said, as he pointed to the white-board. "My chief wants to thank you for wrapping up this high-profile case for us. It will make us look good in the media. How did you get them identified so quickly?"

he asked. Jeannie looked at Pinheiro who said, "We used the resources of the DHS."

Finding three large 16" ceramic indoor planter pots at a discount pottery business, Amy and Joey headed to the warehouse near the waterfront. When they arrived, they saw Billy and Chico carrying out leather chairs from the back of a U-Haul truck. They entered the warehouse which had a larger conference room badly in need of repair. The curved walnut desks were already in place when Chico and Billy placed the chairs into their positions. Joey carried two of the ceramic pots while Amy carried the third into the warehouse. They placed them in front of the two large desks so the blast radius would have maximum effect. "We forgot flowers," Amy said. "No, we will buy some on the night the court meets and after I pick up the "product" from my friend," Joey responded. All in all, Joey felt the court setup looked fine for what he had planned for the judges.

Almost on cue, Joey received a call from Judge Silverman inquiring if the new Star Chamber would be functional in three days. Joey confirmed that it would be ready for them. Silverman asked Joey to follow the court's previous procedures and notify the other members of the Star Chamber regarding the day, time, and location. Joey entered the conference room and signaled the other member of the SDL to be quiet as he began calling the magistrates. All of the judges acknowledged the needed information and stated that they would be there. In three days, Joey and the remaining members of the Sons and Daughters of Liberty would get their revenge once and for all.

The next day, Lomax assembled everyone back in the briefing room after Darcy and Burk told him that they had some background information for the team. "Ok, here we go," said Burk to an audience of Jeannie, Lomax, Pinheiro, and Ismail. Darcy was already up front standing next to Burk. "Joey's, full name is Joseph Alan Rogers, a former sergeant with Delta Force. He has a clean DD214 after serving six years in the Army. We didn't find too much about his activities after leaving the military, but down the road he hooked up with William Wagner known to his friends as Billy. The two of them were arrested in Newport Beach after they had successfully robbed a bank. We are still waiting for the complete reports from Newport PD and our office down there. They were both found guilty and served four years of an eight-year sentence. By the way, we have no current addresses on any of them.

Darcy then jumped in. "We think we may have the motivation that attracted Joey to the Star Chamber. Miranda secured his juvenile records. As a juvenile he was technically never arrested but spent a considerable amount of time in foster care. His father was an alcoholic and abused Joey's mother routinely. When Joey was seven years old, his father severely injured his mother, placing her in the hospital. His father was arrested and since there was no one to care for Joey, he was placed in child protective service. His mom got a restraining order, but every time she called the police, they talked her out of prosecuting, telling her it was a waste of time. His mother returned to Joey's dad who promised to seek counseling and give up booze. We have all heard the story, right?" she asked, not expecting a reply. "Two years later, his father came home in a drunken rage and this time strangled Joey's mother, killing her, right in front of Joey. Joey called the emergency line and his father, in panic, fled the scene only to wrap his truck around a telephone pole, dying instantly."

"Jesus," said Ismail. "At seven years old?"

Darcy continued. "He spent time with several different foster parents but could not bond with any of them, until he was placed in the home of Mr. and Mrs. Gillingham who lost their only son in Viet Nam. He was a former Green Beret. Mr. Gillingham had also served in the military and ran the household in a similar fashion that seemed to be a good fit for Joey leading him to enlist in the Army."

"Makes sense," said Lomax. "As a kid he sees his dad beat the hell out of his mom, but when the cops arrive, his father is above the law, and nothing happens until it is too late."

Darcy moved on to the next photo on the whiteboard. "Armando Fernandez has several driving citations, mostly speed, and nothing major. He ran with the Hells Angels but was never sponsored by the gang, so he moved on. His nickname is Chico and he comes from a large Mexican family. His parents are illegals coming to the U.S. over thirty years ago, so, being born in the states, he is a citizen. He has held jobs mostly working warehouse jobs like Home Depot, Lowes, or auto body painting.

Amy Nelson is the youngest member of the SDL. She was a habitual runaway in and out of juvenile hall in Oakland. Drugs, alcohol use, and generally acting out describes her. While living on the street she sold her body for money or scrounged dumpsters for food. How she became associated with the SDL, we do not know yet." With that, Burk looked at Darcy who continued.

"Sandi Osborne, spelled on her birth certificate with an i instead of a y, and Victoria Reynold, Vicki, have arrest convictions stemming from campus uprisings on the campus of the University of California, Berkeley as well as other institutions of higher learning. She met Vicki while in college and friends indicated that they are lovers. Most of their charges were for vandalism, assault, and public urination, peeing on signs announcing an event that they opposed. On one occasion however, the two of them hooked up with a professor and tried to blackmail him. They were both arrested, but the DA dropped the charge when the professor changed his mind about pressing charges. It appears that Vicki has never held a job nor ever filed income tax. She was a professional student.

Sandi comes from a wealthy family which she rejected. Her parents have not seen her for years and have no idea where she is. What is still missing is how Joey recruited them to become members of the SDL."

Burk took over. "That brings us to the final member of the SDL, William Wagner known to his friends as Billy. As we said earlier, Billy and Joey pulled off a daring bank robbery in Southern California, specifically Newport Beach. According to the police report we obtained late yesterday, they had planned the heist for two weeks. They would have escaped except their getaway car, get this, ran out of gas while the police were in pursuit. They tried to escape on foot. Can't hide very well from a copter and they were both caught. "Like they say, we only catch the dumb ones," Ismail said.

Burk finished up saying that they were both found guilty and served four years of an eight-year sentence. "By the way, we have no current addresses on any of the SDL members yet."

"We do have addresses on known associates, relatives, etc. and our collogues, including the SFPD are tracking them down," Jeannie said to the assembled group. "But for right now, we are chasing paper trails.

Chapter Seventeen

Joey placed the two bombs on the bottom of the two ceramic planter pots followed by Amy inserting fresh flowers they bought from a local grocery store. Joey stood back, placing himself dead center in front of the two curved desks and admired the staging of the flowers. "Freshly cut flowers for their funerals," he thought as he glanced at his watch. He made sure there was power from the generator outback of the warehouse for the laptop the justices would use to present their cases. Everything was set. He told the girls that they can take the van and return to their safe house. He gave them money to pick up some food. Blowing assholes up gets a person hungry he thought will catching a smile on his face. Billy and Chico would be parked several blocks away in their second car and would pick up Joey after the explosion was heard.

First to arrive was Judge Roberts. He nodded at Joey who escorted him into the Star Chamber. Roberts put on his black robe and checked out the conference room. Judges Kavanaugh and Kalford arrived within minutes of each other. Kalford, seeing Kavanaugh enter to the side of the warehouse, followed his path. Judges Hall, Silverman and Henderson arrived in three-minute intervals. Joey re-entered the Star Chamber finding all of the judges dressed similarly to Judge Roberts. Small talk took place between the Judges until Judge Silverman hit the oak block on the desk with the gavel. I guess the judges had decided that he would be the first presiding judge of the new Star Chamber, Joey thought. Joey lowered the lights and turned on the laptop showing a female member of the House of Representatives. Someone booed but then decorum took over. Joey slid out the entrance and locked the door behind him.

Using a flashlight, he walked a block and a half away and looked over the surrounding area. Seeing no one, he proceeded to pull out the cell phone connected wirelessly to the two bombs. Looking back in the direction of the warehouse he placed his right index finger over the call button, but before hitting the key, he said the names of the deceased members of the SDL who were killed on the orders of those justices now in the warehouse.

The blast lite up the sky as is daylight had quickly replaced the night. A brilliant yellow fireball traveled forty-feet in the air which Chico and Billy could see from their vantage point. Chico started up the car and drove to the pre-arranged location where they found Joey. Joey's ears where deaf from the blast but he was able to say with a smile on his face while entering the van, "The Star Chamber will not be in session again." There was no doubt in his mind that everyone inside the warehouse had perished.

As they drove out of the warehouse district, they could hear sirens responding. No doubt the sound of the blast could be heard for miles. Joey wondered how long it would take law enforcement to identify the remains inside what was left of the structure. Doesn't matter he thought. They were moving on to the next target.

Jeannie woke first the next morning with Pinheiro on his side facing away from her. She thought about sliding out of the bed and not disturbing him but then changed her mind. She turned to face him and placed her arm around his waist finally placing it on his chest. She then scooted her waist against his buttocks and quickly fell back asleep. "God, how she loved this man," she thought. Around 9 a.m., Jeannie's phone vibrated on the nightstand. She looked at the display and saw that it was Tami, her secretary. "Hi Tami, what's up?" Jeannie said. "What? Where? When did that happen?" she said into the phone as she sat up. The conversation woke Ricky up who turned on his side facing Jeannie. "Ok, get ahold of Ismail and have him meet me there. We will be driving up Highway 880. My ETA is about 1 hour."

She turned to Ricky and told him what Tami has relayed. An abandoned warehouse on the west side of Oakland near the waterfront blew up last night. Oakland PD found six bodies inside, but they are burned beyond recognition. "It has to be the Star Chamber. They started back up."

"I am happy to say that our comrades did not die in vain. The Star Chamber is no more," Joey boasted to the group. Vicki started to clap with Sandi following her lead. "Now that that if behind us, we can discuss our plans for the kidnapping of Mr. Sadler's teenage daughter. Vicki, what did you and Sandi learn from your scouting expedition yesterday?" he asked.

Chapter Eighteen

J oey was the first to enter the kitchen. Everyone
else is the house was still asleep after a long night
of partying over the end of the Star Chamber.
He decided to take a quick run down to the corner
liquor store and buy a newspaper, so he could read
how the fake media described the event of last night.
He wasn't disappointed since it was the lead item on
the front page.

"Six People Killed in Warehouse Explosion"

The article did not state any connection to the
Star Chamber. It simply stated that an explosion
had occurred in an abandoned warehouse in West
Oakland and that so far, six bodies had been found.
The dead were not identified, and the paper said that
this would not happen until relatives were notified.
Joey knew that the police would have to rely on dental

records and DNA to secure the identification of the dead judges, but he didn't care. He got his revenge.

Returning home, he found Amy still in her panties and white t-shirt eating a bowl of Coco puffs at the kitchen table. Joey showed her the newspaper and she smiled. "How was your run?" she asked. "Great, the air is so clean in the early morning hours. After breakfast, you and I need to take a ride down to Atherton, in San Mateo county."

"Is that where Sadler's house is?" asked Amy. "Yeah," I just want to check it out," Joey said as he grabbed a dish and filled it with cereal and milk.

Ricky was already creating a breakfast delight in the kitchen when Jeannie walked in wearing the sexy satin and lace chemise from the previous night. "Smells good," she said, as Ricky handed her a hot cup of coffee. "Are you going to continue to make breakfast for me after we get married?" she asked after taking her first sip. "You keep dressing like that in the morning, and you can count of breakfast every day," he said leering at her with a hint of a smile.

He plated two plates he had on the countertop and walked them over to the kitchen table. They talked about their childhood, their likes and dislikes about movies, sports, and cars. They shared the same political points of view and Ricky told her that a purge of the holdover appointees of Obama were also being removed similar to those in the FBI. Ricky picked up the empty plates and after rinsing them, put them in the dishwasher. Jeannie brought over the two coffee cups and was preparing to refill them when Ricky took them from her hands and placed them on the counter near the Cuisinart coffee maker. He then turned into Jeannie and started kissing her while caressing her breasts. His hands lowered the shoulder straps dropping the chemise onto the kitchen floor. Jeannie responded by pulling the t-shirt Ricky wore over his head dropping it onto her chemise. She then grabbed the front of his sweatpants and pulled them down to his feet. He quickly pulled his feet free of the cotton pants and their sexual exploration went into overdrive.

Fifteen minutes later, still both laying on the kitchen floor, Jeannie said, "If your cousin saw us now, he would say something like, who's the perverts now?" Ricky started to laugh and then Jeannie said, "Oh my God," jumping up and quickly putting on her nightgown. "What if Delores was looking in the kitchen window?" Ricky started to laugh even louder while getting up, grabbing his sweatpants and t-shirt. "Well, if she did, she probably ran right home and is now giving Mr. Delores the time of his life," he said. Jeannie ran into his waiting arms and laughed almost as loud as he was. "God, we are bad," Jeannie said into Ricky's chest. "Actually, I thought it was damn good," he replied.

The sign on the side of the van read AAA plumbing. "What's with the sign?" Amy asked Joey as they walked towards the vehicle. Joey was carrying a toolbox and opened the side sliding door, placing it on the floor. He then closed the door and looked at the magnetic sign. "People don't notice repairmen. They remember the color of their uniform and the color of the vehicle, but that's it. The uniform can get you into almost anywhere."

They drove south down Highway 101 to Atherton, a very wealthy neighborhood attracting the likes of sport figures, celebrities, and politicians – people like Howard Sadler. Joey told Amy that Atherton was ranked as having the highest per capita income among U.S. towns with a population between 2,500 and 9,999. "Looks like it. Gee, these homes and yards are huge," she said. "Yeah, it is regularly ranked as the most expensive ZIP Code in the United States. At one time Ty Cobb, the Hall of Fame Major League Baseball player lived here. I am not sure if Stephen Curry, the NBA star for the Golden State, Willie Mays the Hall of Famer or Jerry Rice, the 49ers wide receiver still live there or not but a lot of upper-crust people call it their home."

They found Salder's estate and like all the other properties it was huge. The entire estate was completely enclosed by an 8' wrought iron fence. The front gate was monitored by cameras and a call box. Joey and Amy counted three gorgeous German Shepherds running around the manicured lawn as well as two uniformed security officers who were unarmed sitting near the oversized entrance doors to the main structure.

The residence was four-stories tall. Without an architectural drawing of the home, Joey could only guess as to the layout, which was not good when you were thinking about storming the house. They drove around the neighborhood and saw that the adjacent homes also had more than adequate security. Joey decided that the estate was too hardened a target to attempt the kidnapping there. He had to come up with a different plan. They drove through a Chic-fil-A and got two chicken sandwiches and sodas and then decided to park in a grocery store parking lot to eat. "What should we do?" asked Amy while wiping her face with a napkin.

"You and I can't keep driving around the neighborhood in the van. People will start to question why we are there. No, instead, I will have Vicki and Sandi take our other car and watch the activity of the house for the next few days. They can drive around or park and stroll hand in hand. The people who live in this liberal neighborhood would not question two lesbians making out on the sidewalk. Let's get home."

Jeannie showered first and decided to let her hair air dry. When Ricky came out of the bathroom he called out for Jeannie. "In here," she said while looking at her spare bedroom's wall. Ricky entered and said, "When did you do this?" On the wall were duplicate pictures of the SDL with Joey's picture being in the center with strings going to various other pictures.

"Last night, after we made love, I couldn't sleep, so I got up quietly and came in here."

"Did you get anything out of it?" Ricky asked as he stepped forward and looked at Jeannie's work. "Not really, but I did come up with something we could follow up on until we get a solid lead," she said. "What's that?" he asked. "Well, remember when either Burk or Darcy talked about the tragic life Joey had? The fact that his father killed his mother?" Ricky replied with "Yeah, so what?". "Well, here is what I am thinking. Mother's Day is almost here. Somewhere I read where his mother is buried." "Ok, now I know where this is going?" Ricky said. "What the hell, I don't think you have anything else to work on. Maybe we will luck out."

Chapter Nineteen

Jeannie missed waking up next to Ricky, but duty calls, and he had to return to D.C. but would return in two weeks. That Saturday she verified that her request for three surveillance teams would be in place tomorrow morning, Mother's Day. She agreed with Ricky that it was a long shot, but so far, none of her agents assigned to the investigation had turned up anything. Relatives, friends, associates had nothing to offer in their search for the killers. Bomb experts did verify that it was two homemade bombs detonated remotely that killed the six people in the warehouse explosion. DNA matches identified the six magistrates. Jeannie was sure that they had decided the heat was off and to start up the Star Chamber again. She had also put two and two together and believed that Joey was the mastermind who convinced the six judges to attend the abandoned warehouse where they would meet their end. All for revenge over the three fallen former SDL members ordered killed by the court.

Her thoughts then turned to her deceased mother with Mother's Day almost upon her. Her mother had passed away several years ago, but she always placed flowers on her grave on special occasions, such as her birthday, Christmas, and for tomorrow. Fortunately, she was in a different cemetery than the one being staked out tomorrow. She would get up early, miss Ricky's famous breakfast, and after grabbing something to eat, would pick up some flowers and head to the resting spot. From there she would head in the general direction of the stakeout but well out of the immediate area.

Joey and the SDL were gathered in the small front room of their safe house. Once again, he had a large piece of cardboard showing several drawings. "Based on great work by Vicki and Sandi, I think we now have a great idea on how to proceed with the kidnapping of Sadler's daughter. Sadler's house has too much security. Charlotte Sadler attends this private high school. Each school day, she is driven by a chauffeur to and from, taking the same route each day. As you can see, the limo has to stop at this intersection to make a left-hand turn. Next Monday, Billy and Amy will drive the Ford Focus here, making it look like you are having car trouble. When the chauffeur stops for the stop sign he will see that we are blocking his left turn. I will drive up behind the limo with Vicki and

Sandi. Billy will come up to the driver's door and ask if he could make a call for a tow. After the driver puts the car in park, Billy will put one in his head.

Quickly, Vicki and Sandi will jump out of the van, leaving the door open. You two will run up to the right passenger side of the limo. After opening the door, you will grab Charlotte from the back seat. You must do it fast enough so she cannot use her cell phone. If she is already on the phone, slap it out of her hands before she can say anything about what is happening. I will drive up next to the limo in the van. You two will push Charlotte into the van following her inside. Billy will return to the Focus. Each vehicle will take a different route back to the safe house. Any questions?

Jeannie and Ismael were parked outside of the cemetery but close enough that the grave of Joey's mother could be seen without the need of binoculars. About 30 feet away, recently transferred agents Alicia Anthony and Steven Wilcock's had spread a blanket on the grass near a grave and were rearranging flowers they had placed on the headstone. On a knoll in the opposite direction, sat Agent Davenport, sitting on a donated concrete bench reading a book. A half-a-block away, Agents Brooke Adams and her partner Scott Larson, were seated in a Chevrolet Impala in case the suspect or suspects tried to flee the scene. As the hours passed without any sign of Joey or SDL members, Jeannie began moving the teams around to keep the charade changing. By late afternoon Jeannie knew her hunch was not going to pay off and canceled the surveillance teams. She and Ismail started their car and headed back to the bureau. From their vantage point they could not see a male watching all of the FBI activity in his binoculars. "Sorry Mom, Joey said to himself in the Focus. I will bring flowers as soon as I can. I love you,"

Howard Sadler was a multi-billionaire. With a large amount of seed money he inherited from his parents, he developed one of the largest firms that supplied parts for major smartphones. The parts were manufactured on the sweat of third-world employees making $2.00 a day, working 14-hours Monday through Saturday. He and his wife belonged to three country clubs, owned a superyacht, and both drove matching Jaguars. Charlotte, their only child, just turned 17-years old and was a stuck-up bitch having been born with a silver spoon in her mouth. She never desired a driver's license. She didn't need one with a limo at her beckon call.

Monica Stromberg married Howard when she was 20-years old, not for love, but because of his money which, as his company grew, she could spend lavishly. She was five inches taller than her husband, which wasn't saying much since he only stood 5'3". But what he lacked in height, he made up for in weight which was currently at 320 pounds. Always sporting a tan, sometimes sprayed on, she loved spending time playing tennis at one of the country clubs in the area.

She sponsored galas at their estate and never found a cause that she and Howard did not donate too, especially if it generated a lot of media coverage or future political favoritism.

Charlotte was an inconvenience. Discovering her pregnancy too late, she decided to go ahead with the birth to avoid any scandal if it leaked out that she had an abortion. Charlotte began attending private pre-schools, ballet, gymnastics, anything that would put her in the spotlight next to Monica. Monica controlled who Charlotte developed friendships with and was currently scouting what she considered, the best university her daughter would attend shortly upon graduation.

Howard could care less. Trapped in a loveless marriage, he traveled often and paid for the services of expensive call girls whenever he had the need. At one time he had a mistress, but she became too demanding, so he terminated the relationship and gave her some quiet money. "No, he thought, screwing call girls was the way to go. No attachment issues. Just pure sex. Sure, there was the risk of STDs, but he dismissed the worry by having several doctors on standby who would be paid for their discretion.

His doctors told him recently that his blood pressure was extremely high, no doubt related to his obesity. They recommended that he take drastic action and undergo a gastric bypass. Further consideration for the surgery came when a newspaper showed a picture of him wearing a tuxedo, commenting that he looked and walked like a fat penguin. His agent had already scheduled him for a flight down to Cancun where the surgery would be performed in private. He would then stay down there for at least a month, supposedly taking a well-deserved vacation.

On Monday morning, everything was set. Driving the van with the magnet plumbing sign, Joey followed the chauffeur-limo from the Sadler estate taking the previous route to the school. Sandi and Vicki were in the back of the van with Vicki holding the side door handle so that the two of them could quickly exit the vehicle when the time arrived.

The driver approached the stop sign and saw the Ford Focus blocking his left-turn with its' hood up. Billy began walking purposefully back to the limo. The chauffeur rolled down the window and asked what the problem was. Billy told them that the car just died on them and asked if the driver could call a tow for them. Putting the limo in park, the chauffeur reached for the phone but before he reached it, Billy fired two shots from his semi-automatic with an attached suppressor into the left side of his head. Even with the suppressor, the sound of the weapon firing not once but twice, caused Charlotte to scream from the back seat. She had a cell phone in her right hand and had been texting, when the passenger door quickly opened, and Vicki reached in slapping it from her hand.

Grabbing Charlotte's long auburn hair, she pulled the teenager from the backseat into the waiting arms of Sandi who placed a pillowcase over her head. Vicki and Sandi then forcible lead her to the opened side door of the van and threw her inside. They then climbed in and slammed the door shut. Her cell phone laid on the floor of the limo still receiving unanswered text messages.

Jeannie had set her alarm for 6 a.m. so that she could get a light workout in before heading across the bay. But, when it went off, she hit the snooze button, rolled over onto the pillow used by Ricky, and after picking up his scent, went back to sleep. It did not last long due to the vibration of her cell phone. It was the office. "Good morning, Tami," she said. "Sorry for waking you Jeannie, but the SAC has called for an all-hands-on-deck meeting in two hours. "What's up?" Jeannie asked. "A little over an hour ago, Howard Sadler's teenage daughter, Charlotte was kidnapped, and her limo driver was killed."

Chapter Twenty

Jeannie got off the elevator and stopped at Tami's desk. "Any new development?" she asked. "Not to my knowledge," was the reply. "Hey, boss, did you get to go to the gym?" asked Ismail handing her a cup of coffee. "No, I had hoped to sleep in, but here I am," Jeannie said. "So, what do we know?" she asked as the two headed towards her office. "Kid was being driven to her private school in a limo. Looks like the perps had an ambush set up since as soon as the driver of the limo stopped, he took two in the head. The seventeen-year-old daughter of Sadler, Charlotte, was taken from the backseat and gone. Her cell phone was on the floor near where she was seated. Took some planning."

"Witnesses, video, anything?" Jeannie asked. "Not so far," Ismail said. "The Sadler's live out in Atherton and you know how the high-brows out there feel about having cameras at intersections. It's an invasion of their privacy. If the Sadler's were part of that group, I bet they wish they had requested installation of video cameras, because right now, we got nothing to go on. There are approximately 7,000 people living there and the residences are so spread out due to the large acreage of each parcel, it is almost rural. Atherton PD has already formally requested our help and the SAC wants everyone, and I mean everyone, in the briefing room in 35 minutes."

Making sure no one was watching; Vicki and Sandi pulled the hooded Charlotte from the side van door and went into the kitchen of the safe house. They walked her down the narrow hallway to a hall closet and pushed her inside leaving the pillowcase on. "If you open the door bitch, you are dead," said Vicki.

Soon everyone had returned from the kidnapping location and, keeping an eye on the hall closet door, met in the front room. "Good job everyone," said Joey. "Everyone performed with military precision. Now we let time work for us." Glancing at his watch, Joey told the group that by now the cops had already been notified and they will request the aid of the FBI. The phones of Sadler's residence are being monitored and they will be expecting a ransom call."

"Is that what we are going to do?" asked Amy. "Not yet," said Joey. I want frustration to set in with the Sadler's as well as law enforcement. We will wait 4-5 days and then send them a communique. I bet

Vicki, our academian, knows what I am shooting for, right Vicki?"

Vicki loved being referred to as the most intelligent member of the group. "Sure do," she said. Looking at the group, Vicki asked if anyone remembers the Symbionese Liberation Army (SLA) and the kidnapping of Patty Hearst? She was not surprised that no one, except Joey, knew anything, so she decided to give them a brief history.

"The Symbionese Liberation Army was an American left-wing terrorist organization active between 1973 and 1975. The group committed bank robberies, two murders, and other acts of violence. The SLA became internationally notorious for the kidnapping of heiress Patricia Hearst, abducting the 19-year-old from Berkeley, California. She later joined the SLA. I believe Joey's plan is for us to duplicate that famous case with Charlotte Sadler being our Patty Hearst."

"You should have been a professor, Vicki. You did an excellent job outlining our little plan with Ms. Sadler back there," Joey said to the delight of Vicki. "I want you and Sandi to do some research on the whole SLA kidnapping event and construct a note that we will send not only the Sadler's but also selected media outlets. Use some of the dialogue the SLA did during their time of reign. Take your time since it is on our side for now," said Joey. "For the rest of us, it's time for rest and relaxation. With the Star Chamber and now our first kidnapping, I think we are due some time off. Amy, put a bucket in the closet for Charlotte so she could go to the bathroom as needed. She turned on the light and remov her pillow case. Her indoctrination will start this evening."

During the briefing, the SAC admitted no evidence had emerged from the crime scene. "An autopsy was scheduled for later that afternoon and maybe the slugs might give them something to work on. The limo driver was shot approximately 2 feet away, so the shooter was able to get up close. The victim was texting her girlfriend who we tracked down. She could not offer much more than what was on the texts themselves except for Charlotte's screams. Jeannie, I want you and Ismael to contact the Sadler's at their residence. Right now, all we can do is follow the bureau's playbook for a ransom kidnapping. Make sure the two of you are back here by four p.m. for a press conference. OK, let's go people, the clock is ticking," he said as he left the room.

Jeannie and Ismail headed south on Highway 101 to Atherton. "Did you know that Atherton is ranked as having the highest per capita income among U.S. towns Ismail asked. "Gee, aren't you a wealth of information this morning. Pardon the pun about wealth," Jeannie said. "Yeah, if you like that, here's some more. The median income for a household in the town is in excess of $950,000, the highest of any place in the United States," he said with a smile as he concentrated on weaving in and out of slow traffic. "And I bet you still can't find a house at that price."

Once they were close to the Sadler estate, it wasn't hard to find the location since they counted at least eleven media trucks and vans, most already had their satellite antennas up. "Must be the place?" Ismail said as he flashed his credentials to the uniformed officer at the front gate, who called to someone on his radio resulting in the large entrance gate opening. "God, look at this place. It looks like a park," said Jeannie. "Yeah, a park the size of a golf course," replied Ismail. "How much is this guy worth?" Jeannie asked. "Around $3.5 billion," Ismail said. "Well shit, he can afford it I guess," replied Ismail.

Several law enforcement cars were parked near the front entrance. "Shit," said Jeannie. I bet we are going to be boxed in when it is time to leave." They found another uniformed officer at the front door and both Jeannie and Ismael showed him their identification. He opened the door and they both followed the conversation they overheard to the large grand room overlooking a huge swimming pool and tennis court. Two FBI agents were seen setting up monitoring and recording equipment on a table and they both nodded at Ismail and Jeannie when they entered the room. Sitting on a leather couch but not next to each other was Howard Sadler and his wife.

Monica looked as if she had just come from a beauty salon with her hair recently being coiffured in a French Bob style with highlights. She had tears in her eyes and massacre streaks on her cheeks which she dabbed with an embroidered handkerchief with the letters M.S. On the table was a picture of Charlotte dressed in her private school uniform. "Bet she liked wearing that," Jeannie thought.

Looking at the Sadler's Jeannie could not think of another couple more opposite that they were. Monica is so prime and proper. She had had a boob job in the past as well as several facelifts. Her nails would never allow her to type on a computer. Jeannie doubted that her eyelashes were all hers'. The jewelry around her neck this morning was probably worth more than the yearly salary of hers and Ismail's combined. Then she looked at Howard who was wearing black slacks and a black and white designer pullover sweater. He looked like an orca sitting on the side of a trainer's ledge waiting to be rewarded with a sardine for a recently completed trick. His combover looked atrocious and his glasses made him look like a Celestial eye goldfish, or Groucho Marx trying to blow up a balloon.

After introducing herself and Ismail, Jeannie asked the Sadlers to start relating the events of the day before the incident occurred. Howard looked at his wife almost as to ask permission to speak. Monica leaned forward holding her handkerchief and began. "Charlotte is always awakened by Stephanie, our maid. She leaves Charlotte to get ready and notifies the kitchen help that they should start her breakfast.

Stephanie said that Charlotte came downstairs already dressed for school and ate her breakfast. She then grabbed her books and went out the door where Manny, our chauffer was waiting to drive her to school. Oh, my poor daughter, where have they taken you," she said while dabbing her eyes again but, in a way, to make sure her makeup, what she still had, stayed impeccable. "Everyone loves Charlotte. No one would want to harm her."

"So, you did not see your daughter this morning?" asked Ismail. "Oh no, she has to leave so early for school, I was still asleep. Howard and I have tried numerous times to have the school change their ungodly hours of instruction, right Howard?"

Howard seemed startled at being asked to participate in the conversation going on in front of him. "Yes, yes, we have had several meetings with the school's administration but to no avail," he said, looking at his wife to see if he did a good enough job. Howard also stated that he was in his study making phone calls and did not see his daughter off.

Besides Stephanie, Jeannie, and Ismail interviewed the remaining house staff but learned nothing useful. No one had seen any strangers or vehicles in the previous days. They checked with the phone monitoring team and told them to advise them if any calls were received. They then left the Sadlers still sitting on their leather couch and began the drive back to the bureau.

Chapter
Twenty-one

"Charlotte, Charlotte," said Joey on the other side of the closed closet door. "Charlotte," he shouted while banging on the door. He could hear crying and sobbing coming from inside the small room. "I want to go home," Charlotte said. "Please, let me go home."

"Home. Why do you want to go home? Your parents don't want you. They don't love you. You are just a leech that uses the money they earn off the backs of third-country workers who toil away putting parts together for your father's company for two dollars a day. Two dollars a day, while your fat fuck of a father sits on his ass counting the money he makes selling these parts to cell phone manufacturers at an exorbitant amount. You do know what exorbitant means don't you Charlotte." There was no response from the closet. Then the crying started again. "Hush, hush sweet Charlotte. Charlotte don't you cry," sang

Joey into the door, followed by more heavy banging. That was a great movie. Scared the crap out of me when I first saw the flick. Bette Davis was a great actress, he thought.

Joey instructed Amy to take the car and pick up some food for the group as well as Charlotte. Vicki and Sandi were in the kitchen working on the notes that they would deliver to the Atherton PD and several media outlets. Joey then talked to Chico and Billy alone outside.

"You will be the first tonight," said Joey to Billy. Tomorrow night, she will be yours, Chico.

The press spokeswoman, who was an FBI agent herself, tapped on the microphone attached to the podium. "Ok, if everyone can take a seat, we would like to get started," she said. "My name is Special Agent Nancy Hoffman and I want to set some ground rules before I introduce Special Agent in Charge Lomax and Assistant Special Agent in Charge Loomis. Because this is an active investigation, we will only discuss the previous events of the day and nothing specific about the investigation process. I hope everyone is clear on that." She scanned the room, and no one seemed to object. "Very well, SAC Lomax," she said yielding the podium.

"This morning at approximately 7:45, seventeen-year-old Charlotte Sadler was abducted on her way to school. She was being driven by a chauffeur in her father's company limousine. At this intersection here (pointing to a picture on the wall showing the street names) the limousine stopped for some reason where the driver was shot and killed. Charlotte was taken from the backseat and apparently taken to a waiting vehicle near the area. The Atherton Police Department requested the assistance of the FBI which has now taken over jurisdiction." Lomax looked at Jeannie and stepped away from the podium.

"Hello bitch," said Joey who, with the rest of the SDL, were watching a used television set in the front room. "Everyone, this is Special Agent Jeannie Loomis," the one who was always a step behind us while we carried out sentences for the Star Chamber. I was actually in her house once. The court wanted me to see if she kept records at home regarding her investigation. I tell you, she has a nosy neighbor that I had to avoid. She didn't have anything in her house, so we assumed that it was kept at work. That's why I ordered a raid on her office in Roseville, to obtain their records and the laptop of Judge Baldwin. So, you are chasing us again, Agent Loomis? Bring it on."

"Hi," said Ricky after Jeannie answered her phone. "Hi to you. God, I miss you," Jeannie said as she continued her drive across the Dumbarton Bridge. "I saw you on the news this afternoon. You got a bad one, huh?" he asked. "Yes, it's bad. We have nothing so far to follow up on. The suspect or suspects have not made any ransom demands. There were no cameras at the intersection showing the abduction. Frankly we have zip, nada."

"Sorry love, but maybe what I have to say might brighten up your day. I am waiting for my flight to San Jose and can spend two weeks with you. "Oh my God, that would be great. When does your plane arrive and why San Jose?" she asked. "Well I just got permission for the days off and felt that I would either fly out tomorrow and have you pick me up at SFO, or take an earlier flight putting me in San Jose after you got off work. I didn't want you to have to drive back to the city. My flight arrives at 10:45 p.m. I hope that is alright?" he asked. "More than alright. I will be in the cell phone lot by 10:30 so text me when you are at the arrival area.

"Hello Charlotte," said Billy as he opened the closet door. It's time for you to take a hot bath. You must be getting ripe in here. I'm sorry, but I have to put this pillowcase back on you. Stand up," he ordered. She had a hard time maintaining her balance at first but then steadied herself. She started to sob as Billy put the covering over her head. "Grab my hand and follow me," he said. She complied and for the first time in almost sixteen hours, she was able to leave the closet and walk. She could tell she had reached the bathroom hearing water splash into a tub. It was confirmed when Billy closed a door and took off the pillowcase. The tub had about four inches of water already, so Billy shut the water off. "OK, it is all yours," he said.

Charlotte stood shaking looking down at the worn linoleum floor. "What, you want me to take off your clothes?" Billy asked with a lustful smile on his face. Charlotte did not reply as the tears ran down her face. Shouting, Billy said, "take off your clothes bitch." Charlotte jumped at the command and began unbuttoning the white school uniform blouse. "Nice tits," he said looking at her white bra. She then unzipped her blue skirt and let it fall to the floor. She turned her back to Billy and undid her bra strap, catching the bra before it fell and placed it on the toilet. In the same position, she pulled down her panties. "Turn around," Billy said. Charlotte did as she was told, placing one arm in front of her breasts and the other over her vagina. "Get in," Billy said. Charlotte grabbed the side of the tub with the hand she had used to conceal her breasts and climbed in. She then placed it over her breasts. "Shy huh?" Billy asked. "Don't worry, I will grow on you."

Ricky's flight was delayed for forty-minutes but Jeannie didn't mind. She sat in her Corvette listening to *Hitting Rock Bottom*, her latest audiobook. She caught herself smiling and choking up, hearing the true stories of at-risk students explain their dysfunctional family lives and how, through attending a military-style academy, turned their lives around. For some kids, order, structure, and discipline is the right recipe for success she thought. Finally, she received his text and she headed to the pickup spot. There he was. The love of her life.

"Hello, Agent Loomis," he said. "Hello, Agent Pinheiro. Would you like a ride to Newark? There is an excellent bed-and-breakfast there." "It's not the one where the next-door neighbor sneaks around looking into perverts' homes it is?" They then kissed and headed for Jeannie's home. On the way, they decided to stop and pick up a pizza since food on the plane left a lot to be desired.

Charlotte climbed out of the tub and waited for Billy to hand her a towel while staring at her body. "I have to use the restroom," she said. Billy stepped aside and said, "go ahead." Charlotte sat on the toilet and after finishing peeing, wiped herself and stood, reaching for her clothes. "You can put them on later," Billy said, as he put the pillowcase back on her head and led her back to the closet. Before putting her inside, he removed the head covering allowing Charlotte to see that there were five other people staring at her nakedness. She began to cry uncontrollably and freely entered the closet with Billy closing the door.

Ricky placed his small suitcase on the floor near the couch in the front room. Famished, he quickly served himself and Jeannie a few slices of pizza and a beer. Going for his third slice, he asked her if there had been any contact between the hostage-takers and the family since he last talked before he boarded his plane. Jeannie told him that nothing had changed. Her agents and the Atherton PD had interviewed up to seventy-five people, friends, relatives, and neighbors, and they still had no leads. "Do you think it's for ransom, or could it be something else?" he asked. "Come with me ace and tell me what you think?" she said grabbing his hand and leading him upstairs. On the way, he grabbed his suitcase.

Entering the spare room, Ricky saw a whiteboard on a second wall showing a photograph of Charlotte Sadler. There were also photos of her mother and father, the limo driver and most of the domestic staff. Under Howard, Jeannie had written his worth, 3-4 billion dollars. There was another handwritten note stating that the Sadler's have a living trust as well as a 10-million dollar life insurance policy on each other. Ricky examined the display and asked Jeannie about Charlotte. "Does she have a life insurance policy?" he asked. "No," Jeannie said. "We checked." "What are the possibilities that Charlotte is behind the whole kidnapping? You know, she asks for a high ransom. Her parents pay, and then after she gets the money, flees with an unknown boyfriend."

"I ran that possibility through the Behavioral Analysis Unit in Quantico, and they said that it was highly unlikely, but there is always a chance. I don't see it myself. Charlotte is so pampered playing her father and mother against each other to get what she wants, why blow a good thing. But, as you suggest, if she has hooked up with a low-life, who knows. We went through her social media accounts, cell phone records, you name it, and there is no boyfriend that we can see or any red flags."

"You know, sometimes a boyfriend can get you to do something you normally wouldn't consider," Ricky said, as he pressed his chest against Jeannie's back and reached around put his hands on her breasts. "And sometimes, a fiancée can get her boyfriend to do something he might not even envision," Jeannie said as she pressed her buttocks into Ricky's groin.

Chapter Twenty-two

At 10:45 p.m., Joey told the group to gather around near the closet door. He had them all take a seat on the floor. He looked at Billy who was standing and told him it was time. Billy quickly opened the door startling Charlotte who had fallen asleep due to the shock of the day.

"Get up," Billy shouted. The still nude Charlotte did as she was told, still trying to conceal her private areas. "Put your hands down at your side, now!" he shouted. Charlotte began to cry and started to shake. Billy through a blanket on the floor behind the standing Charlotte. "Lay down," he said. Charlotte reached for the blanket thinking she had something to cover herself with. "No bitch, leave it on the floor and lay down." Charlotte began laying sideways on the blanket facing away from Billy and the onlookers, until Billy grabbed her legs and quickly turned her over face up. Charlotte began to scream realizing what was about to happen. Billy slapped her so hard her lip began to bleed and swell up. Billy began taking off his clothes while Vicki said, "give it to her." This caused the rest of the group to begin chanting, "go, go, go."

There was no foreplay, just animalistic lust on the part of Billy. Charlotte screamed and tried to resist, but repeated slaps by Billy caused her to give into the inevitable. Billy stood after he climaxed and found blood on his penis. "Damn, she was a virgin," he said. "Lucky me." He then slammed the closet door after throwing Charlotte's clothes inside.

Ricky did a few things around Jeannie's home while she was at the bureau, keeping a constant lookout for Delores. He had Jeannie bring home some paint and supplies and had already painted the downstairs and kitchen while listening to Fox News on the television set where the kidnapping of Charlotte Sadler was the main topic. He was preparing to paint the upstairs and felt that he had enough time to complete it before he had to return to Washington. Jeannie loved to come home and find a homemade dinner waiting for her, but she noticed her clothes getting a little tight recently and knew she needed to hit the gym. The only exercise she had been getting lately was with Ricky and not the type of exercise she would get at her gym.

"Three days have passed, and I think it's now time to shake up the FBI," Ricky said to the SDL. "Vicki and Sandi made an excellent first communique for the media and law enforcement. Looks very similar to those used by the Symbionese Liberation Army. You two ladies, have resurrected them from the dead." Looking at the two, he said, "Take the car and drive over to Oakland and use the mailbox that is on the corner. You know which one I mean. There are no video cameras there, so they will not be able to determine who put the envelopes in the box. When you return, I will make a phone call to the number the FBI has been placing on the television, and hint that a ransom demand is about to be made. Before I forget. Vicki, you and Sandi need to have Charlotte place her fingerprints on the letter inside each envelope. Ok, off you go."

As soon as Vicki and Sandi left, Joey went into the bedroom he shared with Amy and came back with an old portable tape recorder. He placed it on the table and inserted a tape. "Boy, that's old school," said Chico. "Yes, but very efficient. If we make sure there are no prints or transfer DNA, the FBI will only be able to listen, gaining no evidence beyond the tape," said Joey. Sandi handed him a piece of paper containing what Vicki felt would be an appropriate first communication with the police. Joey looked at it and asked for clarification on a few items, but did not make any revisions.

With the ransom letters about ready to be mailed, he felt it was time to ratchet up the game. He entered the small master bathroom alone and shut the door. He wanted to make sure that no background noise could be picked up that the FBI could use to track their location which he felt was very unlikely. He turned on the tape and began to read from the paper:

> "This is the leader of the SDL, the Sons and Daughters of Liberty. I know by now that the FBI is well away of our previous work on behalf of the now disman-tled Star Chamber. We have Charlotte Sadler as our prisoner who is well for the time being. For her safe return, the Sadler's will give us the sum of 5-million dollars that will be left at a location we will give you on a later date. The bills are to be in denominations no greater than $50.00 bills. You have seven days to get the money."

Joey felt there was no need to redo the tape. Short, sweet and to the point, he felt. By tomorrow all of the mainstream media, the Sadler's and the FBI would have plenty to work on. He and his SDL group can just sit back and watch everyone run around with their heads cut off.

Lomax called Jeannie at home early Tuesday morning. "The hostage-takers have made a move," he said. He told her that several media outlets had received letters and that prints on the paper came from Charlotte Sadler. A tape had been received by the Sadler's also. He asked her to get to their residence as soon as possible. Jeannie called Ismail and said she would pick him up on the way.

"There's something similar to how things are playing out, but I can't put my finger on it," Jeannie said to Ismail. "Why the extra communication with all the news agencies? The tape to the Sadler's should be enough? I think we are somehow being played."

The voice on the tape was that of a male with no distinct accent nor any background noises. He identified himself as the leader of the SDL. Jeannie looked at Ismail and the look each shared was that this had to be Joseph Alan Rogers aka Joey. "How much do you think five-million dollars would weigh?" she asked Ismail. "Gee, let's see, Ismail said, pulling out his iPhone. One million dollars in $100 denominations would equate to 22 pounds per million or 110 pounds for 5 million. If it is in $20 bills, that would be 110.23 pounds per million, or over 550 pounds. You know what?" Ismail asked, as Jeannie smiled. "If we make the ransom in $10 bills, they would have to contend with over 1,100 pounds." Even if they pay in twenties, it still cannot be carried in a suitcase. How the hell do they expect to grab the loot and run?" Ismail asked.

"Like I said, something doesn't add up. I could see them requesting the money be sent electronically to an offshore account. But to physically try to move five-million dollars does not make sense and Joey is very intelligent. Remember what Judge Baldwin said about him. No, he has already made these calculations."

Rap music was played into the closet from the outside all day long. Charlotte tried to cover her ears but was only partially successful. Nighttime finally brought relief when Joey shut it off and opened the door. He pulled out the bucket that stank from urine and shut the door. He took it to the bathroom and flushed the contents into the toilet. Without rinsing it, he returned to the closet and placed it inside. He asked her if she was hungry or thirsty? She said "both."

Joey returned with a bowl of cereal and a bottle of water. "Here you go," he said, again shutting the door. At 10 p.m. he looked at Chico and said, "she's all yours." Chico opened the door and Charlotte scooted as far back as she could into the depth of the closet. Chico shut the door and began taking his clothes off. "Take yours off, or I will do it for you," he said. Charlotte began to cry and did as she was told. She could barely breathe while Chico was on top of her with relief only coming when he had finished and stood to put his clothes back on. Charlotte curled herself into a ball and fell asleep.

Chapter
Twenty -three

On the sixth day the phone, being monitored by the FBI at the Sadler's estate rang. *"This is the SDL. By now you should have the money available for delivery. Tomorrow at 9 am, you will make the drop. We want you to place the money inside a U-Haul truck and park it in front of Abe's bookstore on Telegraph Avenue, Berkeley, next to the mailbox. Don't try any tricks of placing an agent or two in the back of the truck, they will be killed. If we see any other pigs in the area, Charlotte will be killed. Once we have the money, we will give you directions as to where you can get her."*

Jeannie had the two monitoring agents send the recorded phone call to Darcy who prepared it for everyone to listen to in the briefing room. Jeannie had requested that Pinheiro come to the bureau with her that day and offer any suggestions, although he already told Jeannie that kidnap cases was not his specialty. The voice was that of Joey again.

"I still don't get it," Jeannie said to the assembled group which included the SAC. "How in the hell do they think they will getaway? Walk up to the truck and drive off with the money? Even if we were out of the immediate area, they have to think we would bug the truck, and if you noticed, the only thing they gave us was a specific time and location for the drop. What is that all about?"

"I agree," said Ismail. "Something smells. They have something else up their sleeves. Maybe it's a decoy, but a decoy for what?" "What if they have no intention of picking up the money?" Pinheiro said, looking at everyone. "Instead they are just screwing with us. Jeannie already told me about the weight of so much money. I think it is a charade. They are trying to pull your chain."

"Regardless, we have to go along with their request. What else can we do? Let's follow the procedures for a ransom drop. Stakeout the area, put agents inside some of the shops and have trailing cars on the parallel streets," said the SAC.

Jeannie left the group and walked to Darcy's office. "There is something I want you to do for me as quickly as you can.

"What's that?" Darcy said

"I want you to get as much information as you can for a presentation to the team about the SLA, the Symbionese Liberation Army."

"You mean the Patty Hearst case?" she asked.

"Exactly. There are too many similarities with that old case and this one. I remember studying it when I was going through behavioral analysis training at Quantico. This whole thing stinks and Joey seems to always be one step ahead of us. Maybe if we review the SLA and their crimes, we can get ahead of him. Let me know when you have it put together and you can present it to all us."

Jeannie reviewed her thought process with SAC Lomax. He stated that he had also thought about the similarities being played out and how Joey seems to be following the similar patterns of the SLA.

Jeannie, Ismail, and Pinheiro went to their favorite IHOP and agreed not to talk shop in hope that they could clear their minds. Talk involved the Super Bowl trip and the Russian history lesson Pinheiro received at the NSA briefing.

"Jesus" said Ismail. "You are placed in a small room with your wife, daughters, and son thinking you are going to have your photograph taken and the next thing you know, enters a assassination squad who kills everyone. I can't even imagine the carnage, screams, the blood and smoke in that room. Even those asshole gunmen must have panicked when the bullets ricochet off the girl's bodies."

"Yeah, and then, after they recover, their greed takes over and they are down on their hands and needs picking gems mixed into the blood and human remains," said Pinheiro. "Strange times."

Jeannie's cell vibrated, and she answered. She looked at Ricky and Ismail and told them that Darcy completed a task she requested. They needed to get back to the briefing room. Ismail paid their bill stating it was the least he could do for his cousin getting Super Bowl tickets to see the Chiefs beat the 49ers. Jeannie just gave him a push while saying thanks to Ricky.

When the three of them arrived back at the bureau, they joined SAC Lomax and several other members of Jeannie's team as well as Darcy and Burk in the large briefing room. The front white-board was illumined with the pictures of eight individuals – four males and four females. Sitting at a table, Darcy waited until she got the nod from Jeannie to start her presentation. First, Jeannie addressed everyone stating again that this whole investigation seems to have similarities to an older event that took place in the bay area. She told those assembled that she had asked Darcy to do some research and wanted her to share what she found. She then nodded, and Darcy began her presentation.

The pictures of eight individuals were identified as Emily Harris, Willie Wolfe, Donald De Freeze, Bill Harris, Camilla Hall, Patricia Hearst, Angela Atwood, and Nancy Ling Perry. Under the photos was the letters SLA and in parenthesis the words Symbionese Liberation Army. "These were the members of the infamous SLA who, on February 4, 1974, kidnapped Patty Hearst shown here in the photo with her nickname Tania. They were, in short, a band of domestic terrorists.

The leader of the group was this man, Donald De Freeze, and ex-con. DeFreeze was the SLA's only black member. His seven-headed SLA hydra-like cobra symbol was based on the seven principles of Kwanzaa each head representing a principle. I won't go into that since I don't think it is relevant at this stage. Anyway, The SLA formed as a result of the prison visitation programs of the radical left-wing group Venceremos Organization and a group known as the Black Cultural Association in Soledad prison.

The SLA formed after the escape from prison by Donald DeFreeze, *alias* "General Field Marshal Cinque". He had been serving five years to life for robbing a prostitute. DeFreeze took the name Cinque from the leader of the slave rebellion which took over the slave ship Amistad in 1839. DeFreeze escaped from Soledad State Prison on March 5, 1973, by walking away while on work duty in a boiler room located outside the perimeter fence.

DeFreeze has been accused by some sources of being an informant from 1967 to 1969 for the Public Disorder Intelligence Unit of the Los Angeles Police Department.

DeFreeze had been active in the Black Cultural Association while at the California Medical Facility , a state prison facility in Vacaville, California, where he had made contacts with members of Venceremos.

He sought refuge among these contacts and ended up at a commune known as Peking House in the San Francisco Bay Area. Venceremos associates and future SLA members Willie Wolfe and Russell Little, arranged for DeFreeze to move in with their associate Patricia Michelle Soltysik in the relative anonymity of Concord, California. DeFreeze and Soltysik became lovers and began to outline the plans for founding the "Symbionese Nation".

On November 6, 1973, in Oakland, California, two members of the SLA killed school superintendent Marcus Foster and badly wounded his deputy, Robert Blackburn, as the two men left an Oakland school board meeting. The hollow-point bullets used to kill Foster had been packed with cyanide.

"Hold on a minute, Darcy," said Jeannie. "Only a few of you in the room received word that upon autopsy of Charlotte's limo driver, a hollow-point bullet was removed with traces of cyanide." The room filled with soft whispers. "Sorry, Darcy, go ahead."

Darcy nodded and continued. "Although Foster had been the first black school superintendent in the history of Oakland, the SLA had condemned him for his supposed plan to introduce identification cards into Oakland schools, calling him "fascist". In fact, Foster had opposed the use of identification cards in his schools, and his plan was a watered-down version of other similar proposals.

On January 10, 1974, Joseph Remiro and Russell Little were arrested and charged with Foster's murder, and initially both men were convicted of murder. Both men received sentences of life imprisonment. Seven years later, on June 5, 1981, Little's conviction was overturned by the California Court of Appeal, and was later acquitted in a retrial in Monterey County. Remiro remained incarcerated in San Quentin State Prison serving his life sentence.

Little later stated: "Who actually pulled the trigger that killed Foster was Mizmoon (Soltysik). Nancy Ling Perry was supposed to shoot Blackburn, she kind of botched that and DeFreeze ended up shooting him with a shotgun.

In response to the arrests of Remiro and Little, the SLA began planning their next action: the kidnapping of an important figure to negotiate the release of their imprisoned members. Documents found by us at one of the abandoned safe houses revealed that an action was planned for the "full moon" of January 17. The FBI did not take any precautions, and the SLA did not act until a month later.

On February 4, 1974, publishing heiress Patricia Hearst, a sophomore at the University of California at Berkeley was kidnapped from her Berkeley residence. Darcy displayed at picture of Patty Hearst on the whiteboard. Around 9 o'clock in the evening, there was a knock on their apartment door in Berkeley, California. In burst a group of men and women with their guns drawn. They grabbed a surprised 19-year-old college student named Patty Hearst, who had just gotten out of a shower and was only wearing a towel. Her fiancé, Steven Weed was beaten up and left on the floor of their apartment. They threw Patty Hearst in the trunk of their car and drove off.

Why'd they snatch Hearst? To get the country's attention, primarily. Hearst was from a wealthy, powerful family; her grandfather was the newspaper magnate William Randolph Hearst. The SLA's plan worked and worked well: the kidnapping stunned the country and made front-page national news.

But the SLA had more plans for Patty Hearst. Soon after her disappearance, the SLA began releasing audiotapes demanding millions of dollars in food donations in exchange for her release. At the same time, they began abusing and brainwashing their captive, hoping to turn this young heiress from the highest reaches of society into a poster child for their coming revolution.

On April 3, the SLA released a tape with Hearst saying that she'd joined their fight to free the oppressed and had even taken a new name. A dozen days later, she was spotted on bank surveillance cameras wielding an assault weapon during an SLA bank robbery, barking orders to bystanders and providing cover to her confederates.

The SLA issued an ultimatum to the Hearst family: that they would release Patty in exchange for the freedom of Remiro and Little. When such an arrangement proved impossible, the SLA demanded a ransom, in the form of a food distribution program. The value of food to be distributed fluctuated: on February 23 the demand was for $4 million; it peaked at $400 million. Although free food was distributed, the operation was halted when violence erupted at one of the four distribution points. This happened because the crowds were much greater than expected, and people were injured as panicked workers threw boxes of food off moving trucks into the crowd.

After the SLA demanded that a community coalition called the Western Addition Project Area Committee be put in charge of the food distribution, 100,000 bags of groceries were handed out at 16 locations across four counties between February 26 and the end of March.

The FBI was conducting an unsuccessful search, and the SLA took refuge in a number of safe houses. Hearst later claimed she was subjected to a series of ordeals while in SLA captivity that her mother would later describe as "brainwashing". The change in Hearst's politics has been attributed to Stockholm syndrome something I am sure we are all aware of, a psychological response in which a hostage exhibits apparent loyalty to the abductor.

The SLA subjected Hearst to indoctrination in SLA ideology. In Hearst's taped recordings, used to announce demands and conditions, Hearst can first be heard extemporaneously expressing SLA ideology on day 13 of her capture. With each successive taped communiqué, Hearst voiced increasing support for the aims of the SLA. She eventually denounced her former life, her parents, and fiancé. She later claimed that at that point, when the SLA had ostensibly given her the option of being released or joining the SLA, she had believed she would be killed if she turned them down. She began using the nom de guerre "Tania", after Che Guevara's associate, "Tania the Guerilla".

The SLA's next action was the robbery of the Hibernia Bank branch at 1450 Noriega Street, San Francisco, during which two civilians were shot. At 10:00 a.m. on April 15, 1974, SLA members burst into the bank, including Hearst holding a rifle, and the security camera footage of Hearst became an iconic image. She has denied willing involvement in the robbery in her book *Every Secret Thing*. The group was able to get away with over $10,000.

The SLA believed that its future depended on its ability to acquire new members and realized that, because of the killing of Marcus Foster, few if any people in the Bay Area underground wished to join them. Cinque suggested moving the organization to his former neighborhood in Los Angeles, where he had friends who they might recruit. However, they had difficulty becoming established in the new area. The SLA relied on commandeering housing and supplies in Los Angeles, and thus alienated the people who were ensuring their secrecy and protection. At this stage, the imprisoned SLA member Russell Little said that he believed the SLA had entirely lost sight of its goals and had entered into a confrontation with the police rather than a political dialogue with the public.

On May 16, 1974, "Teko" and "Yolanda"(William and Emily Harris) (entered Mel's Sporting Goods Store in the Los Angeles suburb of Inglewood, California, to shop for supplies. While Yolanda made the purchases, Teko on a whim decided to shoplift a bandolier. When a security guard confronted him, Teko brandished a revolver. The guard knocked the gun out of his hand and placed a handcuff on William's left wrist. Hearst, on armed lookout from the group's van across the street, began shooting up the store's overhead sign. Everyone in the store but the Harrises took cover, and the Harrises fled the store and drove off with Hearst.

As a result of the SLA's botched shoplifting incident, the police acquired the address of the safe house from a parking ticket in the glove box of the van, which had been abandoned. The rest of the SLA fled the safe house when they saw the events on the news.

The next day, an anonymous phone call to the LAPD stated that several heavily armed people were staying at the caller's daughter's house. That afternoon, more than 400 LAPD officers, along with the FBI, LASD,

CHP, and LAFD, surrounded the neighborhood. The leader of a SWAT team used a bullhorn to announce, "Occupants of 1466 East 54th Street, this is the Los Angeles Police Department speaking. Come out with your hands up!" A young child walked out, along with an older man. The man stated that no one else was in the house, but the child intervened stating that several people were in the house with guns and ammo belts. After several more attempts to get anyone else to leave the house, a member of the SWAT team fired tear gas projectiles into the house. This was answered by heavy bursts of automatic gunfire, and a violent gun battle began. The police were firing semi-automatic AR-15 and AR-180 rifles. The SLA members were armed with M1 Carbines, which had been converted to fully automatic fire. Police also reported that the SLA had created homemade grenades from 35mm film canisters and had thrown them at responding officers."

"Hey, I remember that shoot out. It was on every news station at the time according to my Dad," Burke said. "The damn press and liberal media started questioning the need for so much firepower by the police, if you could believe it," he added.

"I could go on, but suffice to say, everyone in the house died that day either from bullet wounds or fire. When the fire department went through the debris the next day, it was learned that neither Patty Hearst nor the Harris's were inside the house. As a result of the siege, the remaining SLA members returned to the relative safety of the San Francisco Bay Area and protection of student radical households. At this time, a number of new members gravitated towards the SLA. The active participants at this time were: Bill and Emily Harris, Patty Hearst, and a few others.

On April 21, 1975, the remaining members of the SLA robbed the Crocker National Bank in Carmichael, California. During the robbery, bank customer Myrna Lee Opsahl, a 42-year-old mother of four children, was killed when Emily Harris discharged the shotgun she was holding, apparently by accident. Five SLA members were ultimately held accountable for the murder and robbery, but not until almost 27 years later, in early 2002.

Patricia Hearst, after a long and highly publicized search, was captured on September 18, 1975, along with the Harris's and two others, all rounded up in a San Francisco safe house." Darcy turned to Jeannie indicating the she was through.

No one spoke in the room for a few seconds. Jeannie looked at Lomax who looked at Pinheiro. "Wow," said one of Jeannie's new replacement agents. I had never heard of the SLA or the big shootout in LA."

"Hey, with the way education is today, I believe you," said Ismail while smiling. He looked at Jeannie as if to say, well boss, what is next?" She did not disappoint.

"Thank you, Darcy. That was a lot of work you completed in such a short time. I owe you. Looking at the group Jeannie was about to speak when Lomax took the floor. Well, it seems to me that Joey and the SDL are trying to mimic the old SLA from the seventies. You have the cyanide bullet used on the limo driver, the kidnapping of Charlotte, and now the request for ransom versus food distribution for her release. Sadly, I imagine that if Joey is going down this path, poor Charlotte is being indoctrinated as I speak and probably worse.

"Morning everyone," said Joey as he entered the kitchen with Amy in tow. "By tomorrow the feds will have already parked the U-Haul truck with or without the 50-million dollars. Knowing we are serious and out of concern for Charlotte, I am sure they used real bills. We need to watch out for tracking devices inside the money and bags. They probably have agents in many of the shops on Telegraph Avenue and undoubtedly, the truck is bugged. Surveillance mobilized units are on the side streets and everyone is waiting for our next move. Payday, ladies and gentlemen is tomorrow.

But for tonight, we continue our brainwashing of little Miss Charlotte. Give her another month and she should break, maybe sooner. We will continue to fuck with the FBI, but they will never get close to us. Vicki, tonight you and Sandi will introduce yourself to Charlotte. Make it as sweet and sensuous as you can, not like Chico last night," Joey said as he laughed and punched Chico on his arm.

Chapter
Twenty-four

The truck with the ransom money was under surveillance from 7 a.m. till 4 p.m. Jeannie opted for the money to be in $10 denominations, forcing the suspects to deal with the weight of over 1,100 pounds. No one approached the truck. The only activity was a store owner calling the Berkeley Police Department, complaining about the large U-Haul blocking potential customers from seeing his shop. Jeannie called off the surveillance and told an agent to return the U-Haul to the Chase bank where the money would be offloaded.

"You were right," Jeannie said to Ricky seated in the front seat of her bureau car. "They were just pulling our chain. The problem with this case as I see it, is that no one can get a handle on Joey and the SDL's motivation. Sure, greed is part of it, but with the money and stuff they took from Pavlenko's residence, which includes the Romanoff jewelry, hell, they could've split to a country that does not allow extradition. Instead, they kidnap an heiress and play games regarding ransom.

"Yes, he is loosely following the old SLA playbook but like you, I cannot figure out his end game. Now we have to wait for their next move," Ricky said. "Like Lomax said today, poor Charlotte."

"Ok everyone, let's call it a night," Jeannie said into her radio. She and Ricky would follow the U-Haul truck back to the bank making sure the ransom money was secure. A bureau car drove up next to the truck and an agent got out and climbed into the cab. He then quickly got out of the truck and signaled to Jeannie and the other units close by to come to his location.

"I don't like this," Jeannie said. "Yeah, something is wrong," said Pinheiro.

The agent opened the back of the rollup door to the truck and everyone froze. They were all staring into empty space with the exception of a neatly cut square in the bottom of the floor. "Fuck," Jeannie said as she had Ricky and the other agent help her up into the truck. With a flashlight in one hand and her weapon in the other, she advanced toward the hole in the floor. Peering down the hole she saw a manhole cover off to the side and a large cardboard box that had been used to shield not only the removal of the cover, but the sawing of the truck. "Shit, shit, shit," she said as she stomped around the back of the empty truck space. "God damn it. Why didn't I think about that?"

No one said anything. She focused her flashlight into the tunnel. She slowly began climbing down into the blackness being fought off by her flashlight until she reached the floor. There she saw several Radio Flyer wagons, the kind you would see children play with lined up neatly in a row. Taped to one of the wagon handles was a note made of cut newspaper letters, saying, "*Thank you. Let's do business again real soon.*"

"Damn, that couldn't have gone down any sweeter. I can just see the FBI faces when they open the back of the truck and see it empty," Chico said. "Great plan, Joey," said Vicki. Joey stood over all of the sacks of money laying on the floor of the safe house. "Thank you. I have to admit Billy, when you were under the truck cutting away, I was worried that smoke or sparks, or something would tip them off, but that sawblade worked as you said it would. Ok, for a job well done, I think it is time to get some food, booze, drugs, and get merry. What do you all say?"

Amy and Sandi went on a food run and returned with pizza, KFC, and even Chinese food. Billy, still on an adrenaline rush, bought beer and hard liquor with Chico in tow. While they were away, Joey got rid of some of his adrenaline rush by having rough sex with Amy who enjoyed it.

After dinner and a little partying, Vicki and Sandi had their way with Charlotte in the closet. When they finished, Joey brought in the tape recorder with a script to be read by Charlotte. By this time Charlotte did not try to cover her naked body. The brainwashing was taking place, Joey thought. With her breasts fully exposed she started reading the communique. Once she completed the taping, Joey removed the cassette and wrapped it in a brown paper bag. He then wrote out the address of the large San Francisco newspaper outlet and handed it to Chico. "You know what mailbox to use to mail this right?" he asked. Chico nodded and took the small package and headed out the door.

Two days later, while Pinheiro and Jeannie were driving across the Dumbarton Bridge to the bureau, her cellphone went off. The screen displayed SAC Lomax's name. "This is Jeannie. We are on the bridge on our way in. What's going on?" she asked.

"We just got another communique from the SDL and Charlotte. Looks like she is starting to turn," Lomax said.

"Shit. Ok, depending on traffic we should be there within the hour." She then disconnected. She turned her head towards Ricky. "Another tape recording and Lomax said that it appears the Stockholm syndrome is happening."

The tape at first was just a hiss followed by,

"This is Tania. Charlotte is no more. I denounce my social elite parents and what they stand for. I am

embarrassed after learning that my father amassed his wealth off the sweat and blood of foreign works for the almighty dollar. His workers are forced to work 16-hour days for $2.00, while he and his alcoholic wife hobnob with celebrities and social parasites. You wine and dine with your liberal Democratic friends who prey on the weak, saying they care for them, but only to secure their votes during elections. I now have a better loving family. I am no longer treated as a prisoner but as a fellow soldier of the SDL. The silent majority has only recently awakened, but they need to be shown the path to correction – to get back to the rule of common sense. We will show you the way."

The room occupied by Pinheiro, Ismail, Lomax, Jeannie, Darcy, and Burk was filled with silence. Finally, Darcy shut off the tape. "Ok, let's follow procedure. Darcy, Burke, get it down to fingerprinting and then do your normal search for background noise etc. I am sure we will come up empty but maybe they've made a mistake."

"Sounds like more SLA shit to me," Ismail said. "Maybe Charlotte has turned, or maybe she is still just reading what they want her to say."

"What about the reference to the *silent majority has only recently awakened, but they need to be shown the path to correction – to get back to the rule of common sense?* Jeannie asked no one in general.

"Yeah, I caught that too," replied Pinheiro. "They are not asking to set up a new ransom drop. Besides Charlotte saying that she is not a prisoner, but a member of the SDL, what else of substance was there on the tape?"

"Only what you and Jeannie pointed out," said Lomax. Ismail just nodded. "Ok, everyone is worn out due to this investigation. I am ordering everyone to take off early and try to clear your minds by doing something else. I will see everyone here tomorrow morning at 9 am." With that command, Lomax left the briefing room.

"Hey, works for me. I don't need the door to hit me in the ass. I will see everyone tomorrow," said Ismail as he started the walk from the briefing room to the garage.

Jeannie told her secretary to inform Burke and Darcy that they were to go home early per the SAC and that she would see both of them tomorrow at 9 am. She and Ricky grabbed their jackets from Jeannie's office and headed to the garage. "How about takeout tonight?" Ricky asked. "Chinese?" Jeannie answered. "Sounds good to me."

Once they handled the traffic eastbound on the Dumbarton, they made a quick stop at a local Safeway and each created their Chinese meal from the buffet. Neither of them had talked about the case while driving to Jeannie's house, but they both had been processing it in their heads.

"What do you want to drink?" asked Ricky as he placed plates and forks on the table near the Chinese takeout boxes. "Diet Coke is ok with me," Jeannie replied. She took a seat across from Ricky and he brought over a glass with ice and a can of soda. He did the same. Jeannie had opened her plastic container and began on her orange chicken. "You know, we both think that Joey is pulling our strings – that there is another motive in play." Ricky took a bit of his wonton and after swallowing, said, "I thought your SAC said we were not to discuss the investigation."

"Yeah, I know, but don't tell me you haven't been thinking about it that whole time we left the bureau," she responded while placing some broccoli and beef in her mouth. Before he could answer, the doorbell rang. Jeannie looked at Ricky and they both got up and walked to the front door. Both were still wearing their handguns. Jeannie looked through the peephole and silently mouthed to Ricky that it was Delores.

After opening the door, she greeted Delores. "Hi Jeannie. Boy you are off early today. Hi, she said to Ricky. I just wanted to let you know that the film you told me about, you know, *Last Ounce of Courage*, it so inspired me that I took on the homeowners association about their stupid rule on Christmas displays and guess what? They backed down. Now we can display whatever we want. Isn't that great?" Jeannie responded that this was great news but noticed that Delores saw the engagement ring on her figure. "OMG! OMG!, you got engaged. Oh, and to a looker I must add," as she looked at Ricky. " I am so happy for you both. When is the day of the wedding?

"Well it just recently happened and we haven't even discussed a date yet," Jeannie said in reply.

"Oh, that is just great, just great. Well, I must be running along. Congratulations again. I need to get home and tell my hubby the good news. Bye," she said as she began walking briskly back towards her house. So fast in fact, that one of her curlers fell out. She stooped down and grabbed it, and then continued her walk home trying to reinsert the curler while losing one of her slippers, causing her to stop again.

Jeannie shut the door after watching Delores jogging back to her house. "You're in trouble now mister," she said while smiling at Ricky. "What?" he asked. Jeannie glanced at her wristwatch and said, "In about 40 minutes, everyone in the neighborhood will know that we are engaged. "That fast, huh?" Ricky asked. "Oh yeah," Jeannie said with a smile. "Yes, Delores is a one-women neighborhood alert.

After finishing their dinner, Ricky said he wanted to take a hot shower since his back was a little stiff. "Riding in your Vette with those incredible seats, and then switching to the seats in your bureau car does a number on my back."

"Go ahead honey. I will come up after I throw the dishes in the dishwasher."

"You know, if we decide to stay here after we marry, we might want to get a spa for the backyard," he said while walking upstairs. "Oh, that would be so nice to come home to wouldn't it?" Jeannie said.

"Oops. I just thought of something," said Ricky who stopped midway up the stairs. "What's that?" Jeannie asked. "I can see us in the spa with you getting all frisky and sexy and before we really get down and dirty, there will be Delores looking over the fence in her curlers asked us what we are doing."

"Oh my God, you're right. We may have to buy a gazebo for some privacy," Jeannie said. "That might work, but she might still hear you during climax and have a heart attack," Ricky said as he hurriedly headed up to the bedroom. "Very funny, very funny," said Jeannie. "You better run."

After cleaning up the kitchen, Jeannie remembered that Ricky did not have a chance to share his thoughts on the case due to the visit from Delores. Hearing the shower run, she decided to go into her second bedroom where she had her whiteboard covered with items pertaining to the case. She reached into her pocket and pulled out a piece of paper where she had jotted down some on the verbiage from the tape recording and placed in on the white-board.

The silent majority has only recently awakened, but they need to be shown the path to correction – to get back to the rule of common sense. We will show you the way. "Ok Joey, you little fuck, what are you trying to say here?" she thought. She heard the shower being turned off and went to the master bedroom to grab some nightclothes, so she too could take a shower. Ricky came out of the bathroom followed by steam. He was wrapped in an oversized bath towel. "How do you feel now?" Jeannie asked. "That's for you to tell me," he replied with a lustful look on his face. "Give me fifteen minutes and I will," she said as she entered the bathroom and closed the door.

Around 4 am, Jeannie woke up after being inspired in one of her stages of sleep. "I got you bastard," she thought as she slowly got out of bed. She pulled on her sweat bottoms and her SF Giants long-sleeved shirt and walked in the dark to the second bedroom. She closed the door and began looking at the spiderweb design on her board. She saw references to the SLA, the SDL. The Star Chamber, Arson, the Romanoff jewelry, Pavlenko's home invasion, Charlotte, the ransom plot, the tape recordings. She began moving items around on the board as she remembered her dream.

She did not hear Ricky enter the room since she was now on a roll. He coughed and brought her back to reality. "Hi babe," she said as she gave him a quick kiss. "Looks like you have been busy," Ricky said. "Uh-huh," she replied. "I will bring you some coffee," he said, but he did not think she heard him or realized he had left the room. He returned with two steaming cups of coffee and handed one to her. Forcing her to grab the hot liquid it appeared to bring her back to now. "I'm sorry," she said while giving him another kiss. "I think I found something that might help us. By the way, Delores interrupted you from telling me what your thoughts were about the investigation."

Ricky took a sip and looked at the items rearranged on the board. "Well, it looks like you are way ahead of me. Why don't you go first?" Without any further prodding, Jeannie walked up the white-board. "Ok, as you can see, I have moved things around and, here is my reasoning. Tell me what you think.

Joey was the head of the Sons and Daughters of Liberty, right?" Before Ricky could say yes, Jeannie started up again. "He worked for the secret court, the Star Chamber, arranging for assassins to carry out the court's verdicts. To do so, you have to conclude that he felt justified in the actions of the court and relished in carrying out the death sentences. Ok, so here is Joey, a person who solidly believes in the red, white and blue, defended our nation, leans more towards the Timothy McVeigh crowd than the liberal Democrats. Due to what happened with his mother and alcoholic father, he saw that some people are not judged for their actions. Therefore, he felt that through the Star Chamber, he was an arm of the court meeting out justice. What do you think so far?" Jeannie asked.

"Makes perfect sense to me. Go on," he said.

"Ok, things appear to be going along fine for the Star Chamber and the SDL, until Judge Baldwin gets arrested for his involvement in child porn. That had to hurt Joey. Here was a justice of the Star Chamber, bringing justice to those that thought they were above the law, and low and behold, one of their own is a pervert. To make matters worse, the judge was even involved in the sex island escapades. As Joey processes these realizations, he finds out that several of his assassins were being killed from orders of the Star Chamber justices. That was the final straw for Joey. He decides to take matters into his own hands. How am I doing ace?" she asked

"Not bad. I want to see what else your beautiful mind and body has put together," he replied. He continued to sip his coffee while Jeannie was too wired to indulge in hers.

"I don't know how Joey was introduced to Pavlenko but based on what Ismail saw at the crime scene, he had a connection with the liberal billionaire. This was shown on the tapes where Joey was invited into the mansion without question. What I think is that some of these anarchist activities, you know, like the one recently on the Berkeley campus, had to be funded by someone. That someone is Pavlenko. Joey, still having contacts with the remaining members of the SDL, uses funds provided by Pavlenko and there is our connection. During one of his visits, Joey must have seen the Romanoff jewelry and later, the arsenal of weapons that prick had. Joey needs funds and he and the SDL hit Pavelenko's estate and voila, he has money, the Romanoff gems and guns galore." She then paused and finally took a sip of coffee that had now cooled.

Jeannie winked at Ricky and said, "how does it feel?" "Feels good, please keep going while you are on a roll," he replied.

She took another sip, said it was good coffee and walked to the right side of the whiteboard. "Ok, Joey seeks revenge from the Star Chamber for this comrades being killed on orders of the Star Chamber. The Star Chamber was attempting to clean up all loose ends after Judge Baldwin was arrested. That included the cleanup of the last known location of the Star Chamber. He started off with the killings of judges Katamoto and Swartz but, knocking them off one by one, was too slow since Joey had other plans to execute. Somehow, he was able to convince the judges of the secretive court that he was not responsible for the killing of Katamoto or Swartz and convinced them to re-establish the Star Chamber." She stopped and looked at Ricky.

"That ties into the warehouse fire where the rest of the judges were killed off," he said.

"That's my guess," she replied.

"So now he's gotten revenge for his compatriots and he decides to go after Charlotte following a script left behind by the Symbionese Liberation Army i.e., the kidnapping of Patty Hearst," said Ricky. "But what about the ransom?" he asked.

"I think this is all a ruse. Remember the original ransom demand. Millions and millions of dollars. All of us could not conceive how they would move that much money based on the weight of the currency. It was as if he read our minds. He never planned on taking the truck, and that is why he told us to park it at a specific location. He knew that if we parked the U-Haul truck by the mailbox, it would be right over the man-hold cover. I know this is way out there but what if Charlotte is now more of a liability than an asset. You said you could not figure out why he wanted to kidnap Charlotte when he already had all that cash from Pavlenko's mansion not to mention the Romanoff jewels. It's simply to brainwash her. He wants to make her part of the SDL."

"That makes sense since there have been no more ransom demands." Ricky said still looking at the board while walking toward it. "So, what the fuck is he up too?" he asked.

Jeannie stood next to Ricky with a now empty cup of coffee. "Look at this part of the tape recording made by Charlotte. *The silent majority has only recently awakened, but they need to be shown the path to correction – to get back to the rule of common sense?* "Yeah, I have been racking my brains all night long and can't come up with any concrete ideas as to what this shit means," he said. He looked at Jeannie who had a huge grin on her face. "You've solved it?" he asked.

Chapter Twenty-five

Tim was a seventeen-year-old who, unless you counted the many times he saw his sister in her panties and bra, never had anything close to a sexual experience until he met Connie, an inexperienced but inquisitive sixteen-year-old neighbor. After ensuring his parents that he had completed his homework for the night, he met Connie at their prearranged meeting spot, normally behind a large tree across the street from what they thought was a vacant house. What would normally start out with some French kissing eventually culminated with his hands under Connie's bra while she would stroke his manhood until he would cum in her hand. Tonight, both of them were oblivious to what was being carried in the house across from them, since he was concentrating on Connie's hand on his penis.

Finally, his attention was diverted to a group of individuals who had begun hauling equipment into the vacant house across the street. He saw at least five people, males and females, who he did not recognize, make several trips from the van to the house carrying unknown items, other than sleeping bags and what looked like Coleman lanterns. Soon a light could be seen from the interior of the house until someone placed a blanket over the window. Spending most of his time on porn sites and always changing channels when news came on, he did not have much knowledge about the SDL nor the kidnapped Charlotte.

After a successful sexual encounter with Connie, he walked her home and returned to his house. He found his mom and dad were watching Fox News. He got a bowl of ice cream and decided to sit down with his parents for a while. The news broadcast began with updated information about the SDL and explaining their crimes. They then displayed photos of the group as well as Charlotte Sadler.

"Shit, shit, shit", he said as he drops his bowl of ice cream on the floor. His dad began yelling at him for the mess he had just created. He yells to his parents, "I think those assholes just went into that abandoned house down the street." His parents began asking him for more specific details and after being convinced, his dad dialed the number on the screen. After misdialing he instead called 9-1-1. He was so frantic that it took the dispatcher a few minutes to get all the details before advising the watch commander.

While this was transpiring, Joey, Amy, and Charlotte left the residence.

Everyone was in the large briefing room included SAC Lomax. Jeannie with the help of Ricky, had taken the items from the whiteboard at her house and had taped them to one of the walls in the room. Darcy and Burke were the last to arrive, carrying in bags of bagels and cream cheese. Jeannie, seeing this, told everyone to grab something to eat while she was rearranging the items. Ricky refilled both his and Jeannie's coffee cups allowing her to put all the items on the board in the matter she determined without his interruption. Finished, she turned to the now seated group.

"Ok, early this morning, Ricky and I had a brainstorming session. He and I formulated it and by no means, do we claim that this is 100% accurate." "Get on with it. We will tell you what we think," said Lomax.

Jeannie, outlining in the same manner as earlier with Ricky, explained the connections between events and people involving Joey and the SDL. Before getting to the information on the tape recording she paused and asked for any questions or criticism of their brainstorming and conclusion so far. Ismail was the first to speak saying that it all made sense and that they had laid out a convincing story that any jury should be able to follow. Lomax expressed his concurrence with Ismail. Burke and Darcy remained silent.

"Ok, here is where we may have some disagreement. In the last communique from Charlotte, she made the following statement, "The *silent majority has only recently awakened, but they need to be shown the path to correction – to get back to the rule of common sense?* Jeannie said to no one in general. "Here is what I think this is referring too. Remember, Charlotte is simply reading verbiage given to her by Joey. It is coming from him. The silent majority he is referring to started with the election of President Trump. A person running on the platform of not being a politician and certainly not being part of the swamp in Washington D.C. Remember all of the campaign speeches by candidate Trump condemning the liberal left and all of that politically correct crap. The silent majority elected this non-politician who began the arduous task of draining the swamp.

Joey, I feel, believes that this coincided with the work of the Star Chamber and the SDL. Make people accountable for their actions. No one was above the law. In other words, a return back to common sense. Now, here is the scary part. As I said earlier, I don't think the kidnapping of Charlotte is really the endgame. No, I think this last part alludes to what is to come. When Joey says, *"but they need to be shown the path to correction – to get back to the rule of common sense,"* Joey has a bigger plan. He plans on his group showing the silent majority a better, quicker way, to eliminate those that don't stand for his principles." Jeannie stopped at established eye contact with everyone in the room. No one spoke. An eerie silence invaded the room. A few took a sip of their drink. Some placed a piece of bagel in their mouth, but no one said a thing.

Finally, the silence was broken by Lomax saying that Jeannie's and Pinheiro's logic made perfect sense to him but added that Joey and the SDL were still a step ahead of them, especially if he had already picked a target. "You are right Jeannie. This part is scary. We do not know what and when they will strike and on what scale. All of their activities so far have been based in our area, but when the Star Chamber was in operation, they were international."

Chapter Twenty-six

In Jeannie's office, she, Ismail, and Pinheiro were racking their brains about the possible target Joey would be attracted too. The three found themselves in a similar situation when they were confronted with three separate jihadist teams sent to California. After identifying two of the targets and being able to prevent one from occurring, they continued to guess the final location. Fortunately, Darcy and Burke were able to decipher a riddle by bin Laden and with the aid of the U.S. Navy SEALS, they prevented the blowing up of the BART tube between San Francisco and Oakland. In this situation they had no clues, no riddle to break. All they had was speculation.

Jeannie's' desk phone rang. It was her secretary. "Jeannie, the SAC needs to see you asap in his office. If you know where agent Flores and Pinheiro are, he wants them to attend also." The three of them quickly made their way down the hallway to Lomax's office.

After they entered he told them that the Concord Police Department has a house under surveillance after they received information from a teenager, that the SDL in hiding in a vacant house.

"How good is the information?" Ismail asked.

"They had an undercover unit pass by and they saw a van in the driveway and one other vehicle car parked on the street. A records check found that the homeowner lived out of state. A call to that individual confirmed that no one should be in the house. They ran the plates on both vehicles and the plates do not match. They assume they switched them out. They are assembling their tactical team as well as the Contra Costa Sheriff's office, but they said they would hold off making any contact until we arrive. Take as many agents and you need."

Jeannie told him that she felt the three of them would suffice so that it would not be a cluster fuck with too many law enforcement agencies involved. He agreed and told them all to be safe. The opted to take Ismail's bureau car and headed for the Bay Bridge. Traffic this time of day was not too bad since it would be a few hours before the commuters headed away from the city to the East Bay. Ismail switched his law enforcement radio over to the mutual aid channel and the three of them began monitoring the situation from afar.

"You know this reminds me of that SLA shootout in LA," Ismail said to no one in general.

"Sure does," said Pinheiro from the backseat. "How do you want to do this?" he asked Jeannie. "Well, we will contact the commanding officer at the scene and unless he/she requests specific help from us, it's their ballgame. They know the area and it's their SWAT team that will be involved, not ours," she replied.

One hour later, they arrived two blocks away from the house where the command post had been set up. Jeannie contacted Captain Lisa Walker of the Concord Police Department inside the Contra Costa Sheriff's Department's large Emergency Response Vehicle. With the addition of Ismail and Pinheiro, the large vehicle was pretty cramped. After introductions, Captain Walker pointed to a large map of the area with the house under surveillance circled. She pointed out the location of their spotters, sniper units, and uniform officers.

Nearby neighbors on both sides of the street and to the rear had been evacuated as silently and quickly as possible from their homes. Jeannie told Captain Walker and the SWAT officers in the ERV that if it is the SDL in the house, they have firepower that would make everyone envious. Ismail listed the types of rifles taken from Pavlenko's house and a guess as to how much ammo they might have. Everyone turned and looked at Captain Walker and the SWAT commander. "Ok, Jim. Get your SWAT officers as close as possible to the house." Looking at the two uniformed sergeants from the Concord Police Department, she told them to back up SWAT pointing the map as to where they should be stationed. "The FBI and I will be here at this angle from the house. Once everyone is in place, I will call the people inside and let them know our presence." She grabbed the large silver bullhorn off of the table that contained the detailed map of the operation. "Let's go."

As they exited the ERV Ismail leaned close to Jeannie and in a whisper asked, "How many officers do you think are involved in this operation?" "I have no clue," she said. "I think we need to stick together and not get in their way," she added. "Roger that," Ismail replied while looking at both Jeannie and his cousin.

Simultaneously while Captain Walker was announcing police presence, portable high-power lights were turned on focused on the house. "To those in the house. This is the Concord Police Department. We want everyone to come outside with your hands in the air. I repeat, this is the Concord Police Department. The house is surrounded by SWAT officers. Come out of the house with your hands in the air." For twenty-some seconds, there was no response from inside the residence. Captain Walker looked at Jeannie. Jeannie suggested that she repeat the same broadcast, but this time refer to Joey and the SDL specifically. Walker nodded and picked up the bullhorn, but before she could speak, all hell broke loose. Bullets began peppering the vehicles on the street that belonged to those neighbors who had been evacuated. Windows were being blown out. Some of the firepower coming from the house were automatic indicating that Joey and the SDL had modified some of the weapons. SWAT returned fire. Shots were exchanged for almost five minutes until the SWAT commander gave the order to fire tear gas canisters into the structure.

Jeannie and her team saw the tear gas filling the house and exiting through the broken windows, yet the intense firepower continued from the residence. The blanket that had covered the front window caught on fire adding to the smoke coming from the house. SWAT officers at the rear and sides of the house were also taking rounds. The fire seemed to be spreading inside the structure as more windows exploded either from the intense heat of from rounds being fired through them. Smoke was now seen emanating from the vents on the roof of the home.

Jeannie stated that for anyone to survive that long in the house, they must have gas masks. Walker agreed. The shooting continued as the fire found its way to the roof. "How could they still be firing?" Walker asked Jeannie. "They're in the craw-space under the house," Pinheiro said. "Using binoculars, Walker focused under the house and said that Pinheiro was correct. That is where the shots are coming from. "All units, the suspects are under the house. Focus on those locations." It seemed that after Walker's announcement, the exchange of firepower increased.

Suddenly a person covered in a blanket which was on fire, exited the house and began running towards the direction of Jeannie, Walker, Ismail, and Pinheiro. The individual continued to shoot their weapon which was on automatic. Bang, bang, bang, bang came the shots in rapid succession. Bullets struck the sides and windows of the car where Jeannie and her team were located. SWAT returned fire and quickly the aggressor was on the ground with the blanket still burning.

Walker heard a scream and turned to see Jeannie on her knees next to Pinheiro. Ismail turned and saw that his cousin had taken a hit. Blood was coming from his neck region as well as the side of his right chest area. At least one wound had come from the side under his vest. Jeannie applied pressure to the neck wound as Ismail tried to get leverage under the vest to do the same. "We need paramedics Code 3," Jeannie screamed. Walker noted that the gunman had been neutralized and called for the Paramedics to approach from a certain location away from any more stray bullets. The gunfire from the house had stopped as did returning fire. The structure was fully engulfed and the fire department made no effort to stop it since the house was starting to collapse on itself.

Paramedics arrived and had to forcible remove Jeannie and Ismail to care for Pinheiro who was unconscious. Jeannie watched as they took his vitals and inserted an IV into his arm. As they placed him on a gurney and strapped him in, Jeannie told Ismail that she would be going with the paramedics and to call the SAC and fill him in. Jeannie asked the paramedics what hospital they would be taking Ricky and gave that location to Ismail. She followed Pinheiro into the ambulance and held his hand talking to him as the paramedic continued to apply trauma aid based on the instructions he was receiving from the hospital staff via radio.

Chapter
Twenty-seven

The Concord Fire Department and Contra Costa fire marshal continued their investigation of the burned down remains of the house in Concord. Three bodies were recovered inside the crawlspace. The person who had exited the structure in a blanket and shot dead on the lawn, was identified as a woman. Her charred remains had been taken by the Contra Costa Coroner's office the night of the shooting. He had returned to the scene the next morning to take over the removal of the remaining dead. Those found in the crawlspace were burnt beyond recognition. It would take DNA analysis several days to determine that the bodies were that of Billy, Chico, Vicki, and Sandi. Vicki was the one who came rushing out of the residence in a blanket. None of the bodies appeared to be Joey, his girlfriend Amy, nor Charlotte. The search went on for the fugitives.

Two days later, Patrolwoman Alice Bettencourt was on routine patrol in the Haight Ashberry district of San Francisco. Her attention was diverted to the rear license plate on a faded blue Honda Civic being driven by a woman with a male in the passenger seat. The license plate was dangling from a clothes hanger used to attach it to the vehicle. After several attempts of trying to read the waving license plate, she was able to gather the total plate number and called it in for wants and warrants. Dispatch notified her that there were no wants or warrants on a 2010 Dodge Caravan. She notified dispatch that these plates were on a wrong vehicle and that she would be making a vehicle stop near the next intersection. Before she could activate her lights and turn on her siren, the vehicle came to a sudden halt and the female driver jumped out of the vehicle displaying a handgun. Almost simultaneously she fired three rounds at the officer shattering the patrol car's windshield. Slamming on her brakes and taking a barricade position behind her open driver's door, Bettencourt began returning fire. Her first-round hit the female in the mouth area snapping her head back. The second round hit center mass and the female fell to the ground. Bettencourt did not notice that a male passenger had jumped out the vehicle and ran into a side alley away from the scene.

As other units with their sirens blaring approached the location of the car stop, Bettencourt remained with her gun focused on the vehicle and body on the street.

When backup arrived, they all cautiously approached the vehicle. She bent down over the female gunman and checked her pulse after first kicking the handgun a distance away. She found no pulse. Still having hearing loss from the shoot-out and the associated adrenaline rush, she slowly could discern the sound of a female crying from the back seat of the Honda. She stood up, pointed her weapon at the vehicle and continued her approach. Being positive the crying was coming from the rear seat, she pointed her weapon in that direction and told the individual to sit up showing her hands.

"Don't shoot, don't shoot," said a female who slowly sat up in the backseat. "I'm Tania, I mean I'm Charlotte. Please don't shoot." Bettencourt seeing other units arrive at the scene and drawing their weapons, told them to hold since there was a female in the backseat. She ordered the female to put both hands outside the rolled down rear window and then to slowly, with one hand, to open the door. The door opened. "Please don't shoot me," the female said again.

"Come out slowly showing your hands at all times," Bettencourt commanded. The female complied.

Bettencourt instantly recognized Charlotte who stood facing her. Bettencourt told her to place her hands behind her head and interlace their fingers. "I don't have a weapon. Please don't shoot me," Charlotte said. At that time Charlotte urinated in her blue jeans which collected at her feet. Bettencourt ordered her to the ground and then a second officer approached cuffing the teenager. "Who was in the car with you?" Bettencourt asked. "Amy and Joey. Amy was the driver," she answered. On her radio, Officer Bettencourt indicated that one female was down and in custody and the last known location of the fleeing Joey to all units in the area. He would not be found.

The Sadler's tried to use all of their political clout to gain the release of their daughter but to no avail. Although she had not participated in any crimes law enforcement might consider charging her with, they still needed to gather as much information as possible in an attempt to locate Joey. Late that evening after a marathon interview, the district attorneys of Contra Costa County and federal prosecutors allowed the release of Charlotte. Should Joey be captured, she would be required to retell her story in a courtroom. Her nightmare would never leave her.

As firefighter Alex Mendoza stirred the dying embers to make sure no hots spots could flare up, he found a metal box. He pulled it from the debris and opened it. As soon as he saw the contents, he called his battalion chief Anthony Stewart over and showed him the box and the jewelry inside. "Wow," Stewart said, "We need to get the Sheriff's department over here.

The jewelry found its way to the Department of Homeland Security and the FBI. The President was advised during his morning briefing and decided with his aides, that a photo op was warranted. The following week, Lomax and Ismail were sitting in the Oval Office with the President. "I understand that Agent Loomis is at the bedside of DHS Agent Pinheiro. Please tell her that he is in the prayers of both me and the First Lady," said the President as the door to the Oval Office opened. Everyone focused on Vasili Sokalov from the Russian State Department as he entered the room followed by several film teams from the big media stations with Fox News front and center. On the President's desk was the chard metal box.

The President stood and walked around his desk to shake hands with Sokalov. While the cameras rolled, the President opened the box displaying the stolen Romanoff jewelry to both Sokalov and the media. After a few minutes, he handed the box to Sokalov saying, "I hope this can bring some sort of closure for your country and the remaining relatives of Czar Nicholas II."

After a long flight home to Mother Russia the next day, Sokalov met with his supervisor showing him the returned jewelry items. "Putin wants to also hold a press conference similar to the American President and show off the Romanoff pieces. He will put all the items including these on display."

The alarm went off in the segregation section of the federal maximum-security area. Officers ran to the area and found cell 321 open. As they got closer, they saw Officer Lake trying to remove a shirt wrapped around the neck of Baldwin who was laying on the floor near his bed with his head moving back and forth to the movement of Lake. Baldwin's tongue was partially extended out of his lips and his eyes were open. "He's gone," said Lake as he looked at the other office entering the room and several standing outside the cell. A sergeant arrived and went through all the motions. No pulse, cold to the touch. Baldwin had been dead for a little while.

Concurrent investigations by the Correctional Department and the FBI found that the on duty officer whose job was to conduct security checks on Baldwin since he was a suicide risk, had falsified his reports to cover the time frame and that he had been sleeping on the job. In addition, the cameras pointed at the cell and hallways had malfunctions and provided no information. The Correctional Officers Union refused to have all officers on duty polygraphed feeding the conspiracy theorist with new blood.

"Shalom," said Joey as he shook hands with the bomb maker who supplied the bombs that ended the lives of the judges of the Star Chamber. "Shalom," was the reply. "I hope you were pleased with the results of my supplies I gave you." "Very much so," said Joey. "It was because of your product that I came to seek you out again."

"Come, let us have some tea." They entered his garage area and Joey took a seat opposite his host. After pouring each a cup of tea, Joey was asked what product he was looking for. Joey told him that he again wished to purchase several blocks of explosives similar to that used prior that eliminated the Star Chamber, but he said he needed something special this time.

"What do you request my brother?" the host asked.

Joey pulled from his pocket a small piece of paper containing writing and handed it to his host. The host looked at it and then back to Joey. "What you request will be very hard to obtain. It is kept in a Level Four containment area due to its deadliness. Are you sure you want this?" Before Joey could respond, the host went on saying, "This item is a thousand times if not more, deadlier than the recent Corona-virus pandemic. There is no treatment for this. None. And, even if I could obtain this, how will you disperse it?" His eyes returned to the piece of paper.

"I realize how hard it might be to collect the amount of this item I will need to carry out my plan, but I will pay you very well for your procurement. But, not only do I need this item in these quantities, I also need for you to find a qualified expert who can weaponize it as an aerosol and I need it by the date on the bottom of the paper." He pulled a large envelope from his back pocket and handed it to his host. "Here my brother is $100,000 to get started. Once you have obtained the item, let me know and I will pay you what you and the chemist are due for your efforts." Joey then stood and was about to shake hands with his host, but his host raised his right hand and said, I need to request one thing myself brother." "What is that?" Joey asked. "I want to know where my family and I should be when this item is released." "Not a problem and with that Joey left without shaking hands. The host sat back down, poured himself more tea and again focused on the paper he was holding.

Jeannie had been staying at the hospital almost non-stop with an occasional break given by Ismail so that she could go to a cheap motel, take a shower and get some food and rest. Rest did not come easy nor did she have an appetite, but her body needed something to survive. Early the next morning she was back by Ricky's side relieving Ismail. After an hour, Jeannie decided to go down to the cafeteria and get a cup of coffee. She gave Ricky a kiss on his forehead before leaving the room. He had been placed in a coma shortly after arriving at the ICU.

She refilled her cup and began walking back to Ricky's room. A female doctor approached Ricky's room the same time as Jeannie. Jeannie quickly walked towards the doctor shortening the distance between the two. "How is he doing?" she asked. "Let's sit down," the doctor said in a fashion that alerted Jeannie it was bad news. They walked to the waiting room area and took seats. "He's a fighter, but we need to go back in and see where he is bleeding. His blood pressure is very weak and he flatlined last night, but we got him back. Ismail did not tell Jeannie when she relieved him.

"Doctor," Jeannie said wiping tears and mascara from her cheeks. "Is he going to make it?" "Right now, the best I can say is that he has a 50-50 chance," came the reply.